MW00627850

THE LONGSHOT

A CHANCE HARDWAY CRIME ACTION SERIES

MICHAEL MERSON

THE LONGSHOT

PART I

PROLOGUE
WORK

Ken Davenport arrived in Las Vegas just before the dinner hour on a flight from Dallas. He took a cab to the hotel and checked in at the Galleria Hotel and Casino's front desk. The hotel receptionist, Tonya, was polite and accommodating to the senator's requests, as usual. Soon, she had Austin, a young bellman, escorting the sixty-year-old Texan and his luggage to a suite on the thirty-fifth floor.

Ken followed the bellman through the hotel lobby toward the elevators. As he walked, he admired the beautiful paintings, sculptures, and other works of art exhibited throughout the hotel. The Galleria Hotel and Casino had some of the most beautiful pieces of art in their possession. The owner, Trevor Collins, used his inheritance to purchase some of the most valuable art collections from around the world that he proudly displayed for his guests to enjoy, just as he did once a week when he strolled through his hotel in the early morning hours.

Austin placed the senator's luggage in the closet and the key card on the table and then walked out of the suite once Mr. Davenport handed him twenty dollars. As Austin walked down the hallway back toward the elevators, he passed Tonya, the receptionist, who smiled at him. Austin smiled back, and a few seconds later, he heard her behind him, opening the door to the suite that was next to Senator Davenport. Austin stopped, turned around after he heard the door shut, and then walked over to the suite. He stood at the door quietly and listened

"I'm all set to go," an unknown woman spoke on the other side of the door.

"Me too. She's on her way up," Tonya replied back.

The young bellman stood there for a minute but heard nothing more except mumbled voices. The people inside seemed to have moved farther into the room, away from the door. Austin shrugged it off and continued back down the hall. When he got to the elevator, he pressed the button and waited patiently for the doors to open.

Moments later, the bell rang, and the doors opened. There, standing in front of Austin, was the most beautiful woman he had ever seen in his life. She was a petite brunette with curves in all the right places. She looked at the young bellman and smiled. Austin quickly backed up and allowed the woman to exit. The brunette continued to hold her gaze on the young man, and when she got close to him, she ran her hand along his cheek, winked, and brushed her hip against his leg before walking away. Austin watched her until she was out of his view. He then got on the elevator and thought about how sexy she looked in her flower-patterned dress, high heels, and pearl necklace. Her attire was somewhat reminiscent of how a woman from the 1950s had dressed.

The brunette enjoyed teasing men, especially good-looking men, like the bellman. Her name was Skylar, and she had come to the Galleria to meet one of her regulars. Ken was always nice to Skylar, and he paid her well for her time and for his bizarre fetish, of course. Ken was only one of Skylar's regulars. She had many. The alluring twenty-eight-year-old had come to Las Vegas two years ago for a new start in life after graduating

3

from college with her MBA. She applied for employment at numerous places but kept getting turned down because she had no experience. After six months, she was out of money and desperate. One night, while sitting at a bar in one of the Strip's casinos, she met an attractive woman named Ava. After a few drinks, the two shared insights into each other's lives, and that was when Ava confessed, she was an escort. She also told Skylar how much money she got paid, and that motivated Skylar even more to take out her own ad online.

Senator Ken Davenport had changed his clothes and was waiting impatiently for Skylar to arrive. The senator was in town to meet with some businessmen, but first, he wanted to play. The Texas senator hoped the overnight trip to Las Vegas would be one of both pleasure and business. The men who Davenport was meeting needed his support for their new oil refinery that they wished to build in West Texas. They required his support soon because another refinery, their competition, already had approval and was beginning construction in six months.

Skylar stood outside the suite door. She looked down at her phone and opened the text she had just received. She read it, placed the phone back into her purse, and knocked on the door. Ken Davenport rushed to the door, looked through the peephole, and opened it partially after seeing Skylar standing there.

"Give me two minutes and then come in, darlin'," Ken said.

"I know the drill, baby," Skylar replied.

Ken rushed to the bed and lay on top of it. The two minutes seemed like a decade, but the excitement was exhilarating to him. He could barely control himself. He was ready, and when he heard Skylar's footsteps on the carpet, he began acting out his fantasy.

Tonya stood there in the hotel suite next to Rebecca Hicks,

4

a private investigator. Hicks had been hired to get Senator Ken Davenport on video, playing out his sexual fantasy. The people who wanted the footage were paying a lot of money for it. Rebecca had turned the job down three times. The client, who only communicated with her through emails, kept increasing the offer until he or she came to a sum Rebecca couldn't refuse, plus her expenses. Tonya was part of the "plus expenses." After all, Tonya was the one who put Senator Davenport in the room with Rebecca's hidden cameras. Like Rebecca, Tonya had a price, and that price was ten thousand dollars, which was about ten percent of what Rebecca was getting paid.

"Are we really watching a grown man, in a diaper with a bonnet on his head, sucking his thumb?" Tonya asked in a disgusted tone.

"Yes, we are, and now we're going to watch his 'mother' change his diaper."

The two women watched with disgust as a grown man pretended to be a baby. It was like a train wreck they couldn't pull their eyes from. The women were silent. They just kept their eyes on the screen as they watched the hooker come into the senator's room, change his wet diaper, powder his bottom, cuddle him, and breastfeed him while he masturbated.

At about nine o'clock, Rebecca walked into the Broken Cactus Bar on the outskirts of Las Vegas. She took a seat at the bar, ordered a shot of whiskey, a beer, and three street tacos. Rebecca had done a lot of dirty work in the past and was known for not being too picky about what she did or who she worked for, but this job was bizarre. Rebecca didn't know who she was looking for in the bar. She was only told that her contact would find her. The private investigator drank her whiskey down in one swig, set the empty glass back on the bar, and found a handsome stranger sitting to her right.

Rebecca smiled. "Hello," she said, greeting the man.

"Hi, you have something for me?" the stranger replied and cautiously looked around the bar. Chance Hardway knew who the woman was and how she made her money. He also knew the reputation Rebecca Hicks had and the sort of people she worked for regularly. Chance couldn't complain. After all, he was in the same line of work, but he believed people could choose the cases they took and the people they worked for. Rebecca worked for anyone willing to pay her price, and she didn't care what the job was.

"Who are you?" Rebecca asked.

Chance shook his head. "It doesn't matter. I need the item you were paid to obtain, and when I get it, you'll get this bag," he answered as he placed a small handbag on the bar.

Rebecca scowled. "I'm just trying to be polite. I'm Rebecca," she said and offered her hand.

Chance turned to face the woman and in a serious tone he stated, "Look, I know who you are, and we're not going to be friends. Now, give me what I came for, or I'll take it from you,"

The private investigator huffed. "I think we should renegotiate my fee, especially since I have something very interesting on video." She suggested as she placed her hand over the grip of the pistol on her hip.

Chance looked around the bar. He then looked back at Rebecca, who sat calmly with a grin on her face. Chance smiled back. He grabbed the woman's hand and forcefully pulled it off her pistol. He put her in a wristlock, which caused her a great deal of pain.

"Now, with your free hand, reach into your pocket and give me what you were hired to get," Chance casually ordered.

"Okay, okay," Rebecca said in pain as she retrieved the small memory card from her pocket and handed it over.

Chance took it from her, released her hand, and walked out of the bar. As he drove back to Freddy's, he thought back to what Freddy had said before he left to meet with Rebecca to pick up the package. Freddy had been right. Rebecca did try to renegotiate the deal.

It normally took about thirty minutes to get back to Freddy's, but Chance took forty-five minutes. He was cautious to make sure he wasn't followed. When he finally arrived, Chance walked up to the door, rang the doorbell, and waited for about a minute before Freddy answered the door.

"Was I right?" Freddy asked through a half-opened door.

Chance nodded. "Yeah, she tried to change the deal, but I got what you paid for. Here it is," Chance answered as he handed the memory card to the overweight man.

"Good, I'll get you what I owe you by tomorrow," Freddy said and abruptly shut the door.

Chance got back in his truck and started for home. He turned the radio on to listen to some classic rock. Chance knew his deal with Freddy was dangerous, but if he wanted the names and locations of the Russians who had hurt Morgan, then there was work, dirty work that needed to be done. Nothing was going to stop him. He knew he was about to play a dangerous game of Russian roulette.

CHAPTER 1
TWO FOR ONE

C hance woke up to the sound of Morgan running around in the kitchen. He smelled bacon and knew she was making him his favorite meal. He decided to pretend he was still sleeping when he heard her coming back into the bedroom. Chance knew she enjoyed surprising him with breakfast in bed, and he didn't want to ruin it for her.

Morgan quietly walked into the small bedroom in the back of the RV, placed the tray of food on the nightstand, and sat on the bed next to Chance. She ran her hand over his bare chest, up to his neck, and to his cheek. Morgan loved the man he was. Some women like a gentleman. Some women like a man they can control, but not Morgan. She wanted a man who was rough around the edges and unpredictable, just like her man, Chance Hardway.

"Baby, wake up," she said softly as she leaned over and lightly kissed his stubbly cheek.

Chance slowly opened his eyes, pretending to be waking up for the first time. He looked into her eyes as he placed his hand around her waist and pulled her closer to him. These were the moments with Morgan that made him happy.

"I made you breakfast," she whispered.

"Yeah."

"Yeah, it's your favorite. Three eggs over easy, bacon, and grits with lots of butter." Morgan sat up and grabbed the tray.

Chance sat up in the bed and propped some pillows behind his back. She took the tray and carefully laid it across his legs, then watched as he crumbled the bacon, sliced through the eggs, and mixed them with the grits.

Morgan chuckled. "Why?" She asked as she watched Chance take a spoonful of the mixture and spread it over his toast.

"Because it's good. It's how we do it back home," Chance said right before taking a big bite.

She turned her nose up. "If you say so."

The two of them sat on the bed, talking about anything and everything, while Chance ate his breakfast. Morgan didn't know what it was, but she got a sense of fulfillment watching the man she loved enjoy the food she had prepared for him.

Leontii sat in his office, reviewing the monthly profits and losses. He compared it to reports of the past months. He was pleased to see that since he had taken over the Emerald Coast Casino, profits had increased by 20 percent. He was still admiring his handiwork when his cell phone buzzed. He picked it up and looked at the text message. It was from the Underground.

"Shit!" Leontii said and looked at Igor, who was watching a soccer game on TV.

Igor muted the game. "What is it?" He asked.

"Find Luca and Sava. Get them back here now," Leontii ordered as he stood and looked back down at the two men's names in the Underground's text message. Igor took out his cell phone and made calls trying to find the two men. Leontii stood at his desk, questioning why someone was looking for his men, but came up with nothing. *Who would be paying for information on my men, and why?* Leontii asked himself.

"Their phones are busy," Igor stated after walking to Leontii's desk.

Leontii forehead creased. "What?"

"The phones are not ringing. I called their last money pickups, and they made them, but they're gone now, and their phones don't ring when I call."

Leontii's phone alerted him to another text. The boss looked down and saw that someone had responded to the Underground's text message, making their claim to Luca's bounty.

"Fuck! Find Luca!" the boss yelled.

Chance had showered, shaved, and gotten dressed, then got a text message. He opened it and saw an address, a time, and the name Luca. After putting his phone into his pocket, he walked into the living room, where he found Morgan stretched out on the leather sofa.

"Do you have plans for the day?" Chance asked.

"I'm not ready to go out in public just yet, but I do plan on cleaning this place up."

"I gotta run out and work for a little while, but I'll be home early tonight. How about I bring home a couple of dinners from our favorite steak house?" Chance leaned down and kissed both of Morgan's cheeks, where her scars were still healing.

"That'd be wonderful!" Morgan said and wrapped her arms around his neck to kiss him back. Chance walked over and opened the cabinet over the sink, then took out a thermos. He unscrewed the hidden compartment on the bottom of the metal container and retrieved some money he had hidden there. After putting it back in the cabinet, he looked at Morgan once more and walked out.

Luca Kozlov was a big man with an even bigger temper. He came to the United States with his cousin Sava. The two men had dreams of working in the construction industry with the hope of starting their own company, just as they had done back in Russia. When they arrived in Las Vegas, money was tight, and they couldn't find work. Before the cousins knew it, they were working for the Bratva. At first, neither man liked the work they were required to do, but they got used to it after some time. Then the money started coming in, and they gave up on their other dream. Now, the two men were in too deep with the Bratva to ever be allowed to leave.

Luca parked in front of the trailer, turned the car off, and made his way inside. The trailer park was a fifty-five-and-older community close to the Strip. The Gorky family controlled the park and used it as a front for their prostitution ring. There were over four hundred trailers in the community, and the family used ten of them for their girls. Each of their trailers had three girls working inside, making the family a nice profit. Luca stood just inside the door of the main one and was surprised that no one came out to greet him. Usually, Connie, or Momma as she liked to be called, collected the money before Luca arrived and had it ready for him by the time he got there.

"Momma," Luca called and waited a moment for her to answer. "Momma!" He started down the hallway toward the bedrooms in the back. With each step, the trailer bounced.

Leontii walked around his office, trying to figure out what he should do, and then he had an idea. He took out his cell phone and texted the Underground. He informed them Luca and Sava were to be left alone, that they were part of the Bratva and all bounties concerning them were to be canceled.

The response he was waiting for came back quickly, but it wasn't the response he expected.

"No one is exempt from the Underground. Including the Bratva," Leontii read out loud.

"We'll see about that," the boss declared.

Connie sat on the edge of the bed and kept quiet, just as the man had told her and the other two girls to do. He had come into the trailer pretending to be a customer. He'd flashed a stack of hundreds, but things quickly changed when he made all three go to the back bedroom of the trailer. At first, Connie thought he was there to rob them, but that wasn't what he was there for. When he took the girls to the back bedroom, he didn't tie them up, nor did he abuse them. He was polite and told them he was there to meet with someone and would leave right after that meeting. He carried a gun in the small of his back but never used it. He stayed in the room with the girls, kept to himself, and didn't say anything until he heard Luca enter the trailer.

Chance waited in the room with the girls until Luca arrived. The information was accurate. The Russian visited at precisely the time Freddy had said he would.

"Momma!" Luca called once more as he got closer to the bedroom at the end of the hall.

Chance placed his index finger over his mouth and shook his head at the women. They understood and kept quiet.

"Momma, if you're in there, you better say something," Luca warned as he pulled his gun and stood in front of the bedroom door. He reached for the doorknob but paused for a moment.

Chance stood on the other side of the door, waiting and ready to go. Luca slowly turned the knob and opened the door. He then stepped inside with his gun hand leading the way.

Chance saw the gun appear and immediately grabbed the hand holding it, surprising the Russian. Luca tried to pull away, but Chance was ready. He stepped forward, forcing Luca backward and knocking him off balance. Chance twisted the man's hand inward, causing him to drop the gun. Chance then delivered a hard fist to the Russian's jaw and stepped back, ready to provide another, but to Chance's surprise, the man went down to the floor.

Connie and the girls could do nothing but watch the man tie the unconscious Luca up, load him into the backseat of his car, and drive away. When the car was out of sight, Connie grabbed her cell phone and called the emergency number she had been given for strange situations.

Igor answered his phone on the second ring and listened to the frantic woman on the other end. When he ended the call, he looked at Leontii, who was trying to hear what was being said.

The boss could tell by the look on Igor's face that it wasn't good news. "What is it?" Leontii asked.

"A man came in and took Luca from the trailer park."

Leontii slammed his fist on the desk. "Who?"

"Momma didn't know. She said she'd never seen him before," Igor explained as he watched his boss pace back and forth before taking a seat behind his desk.

Leontii didn't know what to do. He looked up at Igor and started to say something when his cell phone alerted him to another text. The crime boss picked his cell up and saw someone was claiming the bounty on Sava.

"What is Sava doing today?" Leontii asked.

"Payoffs," Igor answered.

"Where?"

"He's paying everyone that we must pay to do business here."

"I know, but find out who he's already paid and then go to who he hasn't paid yet. We must find him," Leontii ordered.

Igor made more phone calls, while Leontii tried to piece things together. He still couldn't figure out who was after his men. He knew whoever it was had to have money to pay for the information the Underground was selling. They also had to have contacts who could shut Luca's and Sava's cell phones off.

Chance was sitting in his car with a very unhappy Luca secured in the floorboard in the back when he received the text message he had been waiting for.

"It won't be long now. We're going to go pick up your friend and then we'll be all set for our outing this afternoon," Chance said before placing the rental car in drive and pulling out of the shopping center parking lot.

"Mmph!" Luca mumbled through the gag that had been placed into his mouth.

"What's that?" Chance asked.

"Mmph!" Luca repeated.

"Yeah, I agree. I am an asshole," Chance commented. He picked up his taser, reached behind the seat, placed the metal leads against Luca's ribs, and pulled the trigger. Luca jerked uncontrollably as sixty-five thousand volts of electricity ran through his body for five seconds.

Sava had one more stop to make before he could go to lunch with Luca. The two men had agreed to meet between their drop-offs and pickups around the lunchtime hour. As the short, barrel-chested Russian pulled into the Old Town Coffee Cantina's parking lot, he checked his cell phone for a text message from Luca. Still, once again, he discovered he didn't have service.

Sava found a spot in the back parking lot of the Coffee Cantina, next to the police lieutenant's unmarked police cruiser. Sava had ten grand to drop off with the corrupt police lieutenant inside the building, just as he had for the last two months. Before getting out of his car, Sava checked his phone once more.

"Fucking phone company!" Sava yelled as he tossed it into the passenger seat. He then opened the door, got out, and stretched, and that was when he was hit with something from behind. Without warning, the Russian was brought to the ground onto his stomach. A taser sent electricity flowing through his thick, muscular body for five seconds. When Sava finally felt his body ease up, he tried to stand, but it was pointless.

Chance brought his foot upward under Sava's chin, knocking him to his side. Sava shook it off and rolled to his hands and knees. He stood and charged at the man holding the taser, but he felt the charge flow through his body once again.

Chance stood over the man, watching him twitch. When the second five seconds were over, Chance backed up and allowed the man one last charge. Sava didn't disappoint. He ran at Chance once more, and Sava quickly discovered he'd made a mistake. Chance leaped into the air and put a knee into the Russian's face, finally knocking the man out.

Frank Carter sat in a booth, drinking his coffee, while he waited impatiently for his money. The Gorky family's drop man was late, and Frank had places to go and people to reimburse. Frank owed people who were not the type who took excuses when you couldn't pay, even if you were a police lieutenant. Frank was about to leave when his cell phone rang.

"Yeah," he said after answering the call.

"Has my man been there yet?" Leontii asked.

"No, is there a problem?" Frank asked quietly.

"Maybe. Someone is after my men."

"Who?"

"I don't know," Leontii reluctantly confessed.

"Sounds like you have a problem."

"Possibly."

"Your problem isn't my problem. I still need my money," Frank proclaimed.

"I need to know who is after my men. It is your problem because that's what I pay you for," Leontii said in return, as he believed the police lieutenant had forgotten who actually worked for whom.

"This is outside my scope of employment. It'll cost you twenty thousand more, and I need it and my original ten today."

"Fine. I'll have Igor get it to you," Leontii said and hung up. He hated the police in the United States. The police in Russia were more respectful and knew to fear the Bratva.

The sun was high in the sky directly over Luca and Sava as they lay on the hot desert sand. The men were tied up, sweating, and itching as more and more sand found its way into every crevice of their body whenever they pulled at their restraints. The man who had brought the Russians to this isolated place just stood there, drinking from a bottle of ice water.

"You'll die for this!" Luca proclaimed as he rolled from his back to his side to look up at the man.

Chance walked over to the rental to put his water bottle in the cooler. "Yeah, but I think you'll have to get in line," he smugly remarked.

Sava spit on the ground. "You're a sneak! If you had come at me like a man, then I would have killed you!" He growled.

"Is that what's bothering you? Well, hell, let's remedy

that," Chance suggested. He took out his knife and walked to Sava, then cut his restraints, freeing him.

Sava looked at Luca, surprised. He stood, ran his hands around his wrists, and walked toward his kidnapper with his fist clenched.

"You have made a mistake," the Russian declared.

Chance's eyes turned cold and angry. "No, you made a mistake when you took a beaten woman to the desert and left her there, a woman I care a great deal about."

"She was nothing but a fucking whore!" Sava shouted and threw a wild punch at Chance. The experienced fighter easily dodged the man's haymaker and followed it up with three stiff jabs to the Russian's face. Sava stumbled backward, grabbed his broken nose, and wiped the blood away.

Chance wasn't in a hurry to finish the Russian off. He wanted Sava to feel some real pain.

"I'll kill you and go back for the woman." Sava readied himself and moved forward toward his opponent.

Chance didn't say anything back. He just got ready to really punish the Russian. When Sava was close enough, Chance moved in and caught the man's arm as he threw another punch.

Sava felt his elbow dislocate. He screamed in agony. Chance then put a hard elbow into his jaw, knocking the man down. Sava tried to get back up, but Chance straddled him and delivered countless punches to the man's face.

When Sava finally went unconscious, Chance walked to Luca and freed his hands, just like he had done for Sava. Unfortunately, Luca was an even worse fighter than his cousin Sava, and his glass jaw didn't help the man's predicament.

Sava and Luca awoke to cold water being poured over their faces by the man who had beaten them. Now, he stood over them with a .45 in his hand. The Russians thought this was the end for them. Sava could only see out of one eye, he couldn't breathe out of his nose, and his elbow was still dislocated. Luca wasn't faring any better, as he was sure his jaw was broken, his shoulder was out of place, and he, too, couldn't breathe out of his nose.

"What, now you will kill us over a whore?" Sava asked angrily.

Chance kicked the man in the chin, sending him onto his back. "Strip!" Chance ordered.

"What?" Luca asked.

"You like to leave women naked and helpless in the desert. I think you should have the same experience. Now take off your clothes and don't make me have to tell you again."

The rental took a few minutes to cool off the interior of the car. Chance kept the driver's side window down as he slowly drove along the dirt road toward Nevada Route 160, which would eventually take him back to Las Vegas. He took one more look in the rearview mirror at the two small silhouettes of the naked Russians walking down the dusty dirt road.

The package Chance retrieved from Rebecca Hicks for the two Russians was a good deal. He figured it was a two for one, and that was a deal anyone would take in Vegas. He smiled, then looked into the passenger seat at the G-string Sava had been wearing.

"Why?" Chance asked himself just as his cell phone rang. He looked at the caller ID and answered the call. "Hello, Freddy."

"Did you get your pound of flesh?" Freddy asked.

"Yeah, but there's still more to get. Do you have anything for me?"

"I'm working on it. It may take a few days. Are you willing to travel?"

"Yes, I'll go to them if they don't come to me."

"Good. I'll be in touch." Freddy advised and ended the call.

Chance continued back to the city, he smiled as he drove. He had steaks to pick up.

CHAPTER 2
ANTON AMELIN

Philadelphia has had a long history of criminal organizations controlling crime in and around the city. In the early part of the twentieth century, the city was controlled by the Italian mob. Now, the Russians were in town, specifically the Gorky Family. The Russian Mafia—or the Bratva, meaning Brotherhood— was on every law enforcement agency's radar across the globe. Interpol had countless open cases against the Gorky Bratva, but no real hard evidence to convict them. They were just one of a few criminal organizations competing for Philly and the competition between the organizations was violent.

Chance arrived in Philadelphia on an evening flight. He rented a car and headed for the address he had been given. He had come to the City of Brotherly Love to do some work. Three days ago, Chance made a deal with Freddy to get some information he wanted, but first, he had to do something for Freddy. That something regarded Edward Romano Jr, who was wanted on an outstanding warrant out of Nevada. The warrant was for attempted murder. Apparently, Junior, as he was referred to, tried to kill a man outside a casino one night over a year ago. The victim was Johnny 'The Gun' Adono, who was a member of the Barbano mob. The Barbano family ran most of the crime in one region of Philadelphia, while the Romano family controlled another part, but they wanted more. They wanted the Barbanos' territory.

That night in Las Vegas, Junior and his men had driven to the casino and parked out front, where they waited for Johnny and his crew to come out. At one in the morning, Junior watched Johnny walk out of the casino. He was drunk, alone, and apparently needed a cigarette. When Johnny reached the outside smoking area, Junior had his driver pull forward toward the rival mobster. When he was close enough, he rolled the window down, reached out with the gun in his hand, and fired. Johnny was shot three times, but the bullets didn't kill him. He spent three weeks in the hospital, but eventually, Johnny walked out on his own two feet.

Johnny didn't see the shooter that night, but the valet did. Henry Willard was the valet that night, and the feds had him in witness protection. The prosecution for the county was ready to bring Junior to trial for attempted murder, even though they didn't think Johnny would testify or help in any way to convict the man who tried to kill him. Johnny's testimony wasn't something they needed; they wanted an eyewitness to put a gun in Junior's hand so the feds could charge him with a weapons violation. A federal gun charge would send the shooter, Edward Romano Jr, away for a long time.

Chance was given a location where Junior could be found. All Chance had to do was grab him and turn him over to the state police. The state police would extradite Junior back to Nevada to stand trial for the shooting. Usually, Chance would just drop off the bail skip at the local police station, but in a mob-controlled city like Philly, there was a possibility Junior would find his way back out on the street, especially if someone were willing to pay for his freedom, which is precisely what his father, Edward Romano Sr., would do.

Junior was out on a five-hundred-thousand-dollar bond. The bondsman who put the bail money up was paying fifty thousand dollars for his return, and Freddy was getting most of the money when Chance turned Junior over to the state police. In return for Freddy getting the bounty on Junior, Chance was getting the information he needed for Anton Amelin. Anton was one of the men who had raped and beat Morgan. Chance wanted Anton and the others to pay for what they had done, but he had to get to Junior first. Sava and Luca were only the beginning.

Chance found Rosario's Bar and Grill without trouble. He parked the rental on the street, walked toward the entrance, and casually walked inside. The bar was a middle-class establishment that served whiskey, a few domestic beers, and different meat dishes. The décor was that of a 1920's speakeasy, with its dark redwood and leather upholstered bar stools. Chance found a seat in the back of the bar and browsed the menu he found on the table. He wasn't hungry, but he needed to look like he was there to eat or drink. Chance looked around at the other patrons, hoping to find Junior. The bar fell under the control and protection of the Romano crime family. Many legal businesses were protected by different crime families in and around Philly. This bar was the one Junior frequented the most, at least that was what Freddy had told Chance.

"Hello, sweetie, I'm Wendy. What'll it be?"

Chance was surprised by the waitress who had walked up behind him to take his order. The waitress appeared to be in her thirties. She was beautiful, and Chance believed she dressed the way she did to get the attention of the men who came into the bar. She wore a miniskirt and a cutoff T-shirt.

"What would you suggest?" Chance asked.

"Are you here visiting from out of town?"

"Yes."

"Then it's a Philly cheesesteak with whiskey and a little water to wash it down."

"That sounds good. I'll have that," Chance replied.

"All right, I'll have it right out for you."

After Wendy left, Chance scanned the half-occupied bar for the man he was there to grab. He looked at Junior's photo that Freddy had given him and then he eyed each man sitting in Rosario's. Ten men in the bar were either watching the game on TV or enjoying their dinner and conversations with their dates, and none of them were Junior.

Chance took his time eating the Philly cheesesteak. He washed it down with the whiskey and water. Chance ordered one more shot, a slice of pie he didn't want, and another water as the night waned on. Chance was about to give up and leave when the door opened, and three men walked in. Two of the men were large and Italian, and they seemed to be following a shorter thin man, who was Junior. Chance watched as the three men took a seat in the back of the bar. Junior sat in the corner, while the other two men sat on opposite sides of the casino shooter.

Bodyguards, don't leave home without them! Chance thought to himself as Wendy placed his bill on the corner of the table.

"No hurry, and if there's something else you want, let me know," Wendy offered and walked away.

Chance sat there, took out his phone, took a few more bites of his pie and waited for the bar to empty a little more. He had Wendy bring him a bottle of beer; he needed to look like he belonged there so as to not to draw attention to himself.

It was eleven o'clock by the time most of the customers decided to leave. One man was sitting at the bar, drinking. Another sat at a table, eating alone. There was a couple in the booth across from Chance, having a romantic dinner. Chance looked at Junior and his men and decided on a plan. He placed money for his bill on the table and made his way to Junior and his men. When Chance got close, he pretended to stumble and bumped into the shooter's table, pretending to be drunk.

Junior quickly slid his chair back. "What the fuck!" He yelled as his drink spilled onto his lap. The two bodyguards immediately stood, with one of them bending over to grab Chance, to keep him from falling further onto the table.

"I'm sorry. I guess I had too much to drink," Chance said while looking into the man's jacket at the heavy steel he had holstered under his arm.

"No shit! Do you know who I am?" Junior asked the drunk man who just soaked him with expensive whiskey.

"Yes, I do. You're Junior, and you're wanted in Las Vegas," Chance answered as he stood.

Junior looked at Chance, surprised. "What the—"

Chance pulled the gun out from the bodyguard's holster. The second bodyguard tried to grab Chance, but he wasn't quick enough. Chance delivered a hard elbow to the man's chin and followed it with a kick to his stomach. The bodyguard fell to the floor, holding his abdomen. Junior tried to run out from behind the table toward the door, but Chance kicked the table back and caught the shooter between the table and the wall.

"Mother—"

Chance brought the remaining bodyguard's head down onto the tabletop, interrupting whatever he was about to say. Chance walked around the table and grabbed Junior by the arm, and when he pulled away, Chance punched him in the eye. Junior was caught off guard by the blow, and he stopped resisting. Once more, Chance took him by the arm, stepped over the first bodyguard, who was still lying on the ground, and walked out of Rosario's with the casino shooter in tow.

Chance called Freddy and told him he was on his way to the Pennsylvania State Police Department Headquarters with Junior. He also told Freddy he wanted to drop the rental car back off at the airport and be on a flight out of Philly before sunrise.

By the time Chance and Junior arrived at the headquarters building, four troopers and three feds were waiting for them. Chance handed Junior over, signed the custody documents, and started to walk out.

"I'll be seeing you!" Junior warned.

"I believe it," Chance replied before walking out the door. He knew that getting involved with the Romano family was a bad idea, but there was no other way to get to the men who had hurt Morgan. The Philly crime family was just something he would have to deal with later.

Anton Amelin worked feverishly on his computer. He was under a deadline and needed to get things done. The people he worked for didn't understand delays, computer problems, overseas banking hours, or anything else that would delay them in getting their money back. Anton was an overweight Russian money launderer for Ivan Gorky and the Bratva. Most accountants had an office filled with employees who assisted with day-to-day activities, but not Anton. The Russians insisted that no one except Anton touch the books or know the banks where their money was held. Only Anton knew the passwords granting Ivan access to the money he had successfully laundered.

Anton controlled the laundromats, car washes, strip clubs, and all the other clandestine shell companies owned by Ivan Gorky and the Bratva. The Russians took good care of Anton. Every whim or desire he had was satisfied. The Bratva paid the accountant very well to keep track of their money and to make sure the feds never got their hands on it. That meant he had to move money every month from one bank account to another. He would then change the passwords and access log-ins. When he was finished, he would send them to Ivan.

Anton worked from home, where he used a private server

to conduct business. The server rerouted his internet activities through the dark web so he couldn't be tracked. He also used the same server to skim money from Ivan and the Bratva into his own private overseas accounts. Anton had been laundering the Russian's money for fifteen years, and over that time, he had skimmed over ten million dollars into his own bank accounts. The accountant knew it was only a matter of time before his usefulness to the Bratva ran out. When that happened, he would be ready to drop everything and run.

Junior demanded to make a phone call, and five minutes before being flown out of the state, he was given two minutes. He dialed the number and waited for his man to answer.

"Yeah," the man answering the phone responded.

"Franko, it's Junior."

"Where are you? We'll come to get you," Franko said quickly.

"No time for me. I need you to track down a guy by the name of Chance Hardway. He's the bounty hunter who grabbed me. I saw his name on the custody paperwork. He was driving a rental car. Call our people to find out where he is and take care of him," Junior ordered and then hung up.

Chance found Anton's house in the wealthy part of Philly. The house was a large brick home with a long driveway that snaked up to the side of the house. The front of the Russian's home had bright lights that shone downward, all the way out to the street. Chance parked off the road, farther down the street under some trees. The lights made a stealthy approach to the house from the front almost impossible, so Chance made his way toward the back of the home. He climbed the brick wall that wrapped around the property, ran to the corner of the house, and made his way toward the back door, hugging the outside wall as he did.

Anton finished moving the family's money and changing passwords about an hour ago but had not yet sent them to Ivan. Instead, he took a break and was sitting at his desk watching a sadistic porno on his computer when he heard someone walk into the room. Anton jumped to his feet, fumbled as he pulled his pants up, and stammered as he looked around for his gun. He then remembered it was downstairs in the kitchen on the counter, where he had left it.

"Is this what you're looking for?" Chance asked, holding Anton's gun in the air. He looked at the accountant disapprovingly while the video continued to play on the computer screen behind the accountant.

"No, I was—"

"Was what, about to jerk off to a woman being raped?" Chance asked as he placed the gun into his waistband at his lower back.

"Please, what do you want?" Anton asked. He was scared. He didn't know what the stranger wanted.

"I want to hurt you. I want you to feel the same pain you and your friends inflicted on a beautiful woman," Chance answered as he adjusted his leather gloves.

"Wait, are you talking about the whore in Las Vegas?" Anton asked right before Chance punched him across the bridge of his nose.

Chance hated that word, especially when it was directed at the woman he was in love with. The impact sent Anton over his desk, knocking the computer and a lamp to the floor. The large man took a moment and used his arms to lift himself from the carpet. Chance was standing next to the accountant, waiting. When the overweight man was almost to his feet, Chance kicked him in the ribs and the face, sending the man onto his back.

"I'll give you money," Anton offered as he spit the blood out that was running down the back of his throat. The accountant's nose and some of his ribs were broken.

"Really? Is that what you think I've come here to do, get money for the pain and suffering you and your friends inflicted on a defenseless woman?"

"I really don't know what you want, but I have money here on these thumb drives. Just don't kill me." Anton grabbed the memory sticks lying on the floor next to him and handed them to his attacker.

Chance placed the memory devices into his pocket without a second thought. "I didn't come here to kill you. I'm just going to make you wish I did."

Franko 'Bone Breaker' Calvetti and his two men, Sal and Marco, found the rental Chance Hardway was driving. The Romano family had countless people on their payroll, including people at the airport's car rental agency. One call and they had the car Chance Hardway was driving. With one more call, they were able to have the car's antitheft GPS turned on. That brought the three men near the house at 1616 Washington Circle in the upscale neighborhood of Liberty Heights.

"Which house do you think he's in?" Sal asked as he looked up and down the street.

Franko didn't answer at first, he just looked at each home for a moment. "That one." He finally answered after seeing a light flicker in an upstairs room of 1616 Washington Circle.

"Yeah, that's the one." Marco agreed after seeing what looked like turmoil taking place in the house.

"Let's go and get this guy. We take him, and bring him back to our place, and work him over before we put him six feet under," Franko ordered as he and the other two made their way toward the brick house with the long driveway.

"You still think it's about the money," Chance stated as he lifted the heavy man back to his feet.

"Please don't hurt me anymore—"

Marco stepped into the room, firing his gun blindly. Chance dropped down behind Anton, pulled the gun out from behind his back, and fired from underneath Anton's legs, hitting Marco in the chest. Marco fell to the floor, screaming, but went silent when Sal entered the room, shooting his gun rapidly. Sal's rounds promptly found a home inside Anton's heart. Chance rolled to his right and fired again and hit Sal in the head. The accountant's killer dropped to his knees and fell forward onto his stomach.

Chance heard more movement outside the room and saw a shadow in the hallway. He aimed at the wall next to the door and fired the gun twice. The rounds went through the drywall and hit Franko, who was hiding on the other side of it. Chance waited a moment and then watched as Franko fell over into the doorway. All three of the Romanos' hit squad were dead, along with Anton Amelin.

Chance looked around the room at the four dead men. He knew he had to get out of Philly and get out quickly. He made sure to wipe down everything he had touched, made his way to the rental car, and hurried out of the area. Before long, he was sitting in an uncomfortable chair, waiting to board a plane back to Las Vegas. He took the thumb drives from his pocket and held them in his hand, pondering what could be on them, when his cell phone rang.

"Are you heading back?" Morgan asked. She had called Chance right before he boarded.

"Yes, I'm on my way now."

"Did you have fun with your old army buddies?" she asked.

"Yes, I did, but now I want to get back to see you," Chance answered.

"Good, because I miss you."

"I miss you too, baby. I'll be home soon."

CHAPTER 3
WET WORK

Frank was sitting in his usual seat at the Old Town Coffee Cantina, waiting for his egg sandwich. While he waited, he opened the national news app on his cell and read the morning's lead story.

Three Members of the Romano Crime Family Found Dead, Along with One Known Russian Mobster

It took the police lieutenant about ten minutes to read the news story. When he was finished, he took a sip of his coffee, leaned back against the hard booth cushion, and thought about the dead Russian in Philly. Frank had spent the past couple of days trying to find Leontii's men, and now he wondered if there was some type of connection between Philly, Vegas, and the Bratva. He was about to take a bite of his egg sandwich when his cell phone rang. The police lieutenant looked down at the number and saw it was his commander calling.

"This is Lieutenant Carter," Frank announced upon answering his phone. He listened to Commander Owens on the other end. "Yes, sir, I'll head that way right now." When Frank hung up the phone, he put it on the table, took a bite of his breakfast, and signaled for the waitress to bring him his bill.

The lieutenant had some police work to do, police work that involved a dead body.

Chance woke up next to Morgan, who was still sound asleep. He had gotten back into Las Vegas from Philly late yesterday morning. After a long nap, he and Morgan spent the day together. The two first went to lunch at an old mom-and-pop diner just outside of Las Vegas. Usually, they would have enjoyed lunch at one of the restaurants in one of the casinos, but not today. Morgan wasn't ready to face anyone she knew and could have run into along the extremely popular Las Vegas Strip. As a matter of fact, Morgan had not ventured away from Chance's place alone since she was released from the hospital. Chance took Morgan everywhere she needed to go. Sometimes she just wanted to sit in the passenger seat of Chance's pickup and look out the window at the desert landscape while the sounds of classic rock flowed from his speakers. After their lunch in Boulder City, they set out on their overnight trip.

The couple had driven from Sin City to Los Angeles in about four hours the previous day, and Morgan seemed to enjoy every minute of it. They arrived in the City of Angels at a little past seven o'clock. They checked into a room at one of the more expensive hotels that overlooked the bay and had dinner at a nice restaurant.

The entire time, Morgan thought everyone was staring at the scars on her face. The wounds weren't visible to anyone except for her. The plastic surgery performed on her face was spectacular, to say the least. Chance knew Morgan had other scars that weren't visible on the outside, but they occasionally came to the surface. It would take time for those scars to heal—if they ever would.

Chance quietly picked up his cell phone from the nightstand and browsed the top stories from around the nation. When he came across Philly's homicide, he immediately stopped and read the article, hoping his name wasn't in it. When he finished reading, he looked up at the ceiling, thinking about what had gone wrong in Philly. After rethinking the entire incident he deduced that Junior's men were somehow able to track him down. After a few more minutes, he believed he knew how they did it.

"The rental car," he whispered.

"What?" Morgan asked.

"Nothing," Chance answered as he rolled over and placed his arm around her. He kissed her cheek and pulled her close to him.

"What are we going to do today?" she asked in a sleepy voice.

"Shopping. I want to take you shopping."

"That'll be fun, but can we start with some breakfast first?"

"Absolutely," Chance replied and leaned over to kiss her softly.

The Nevada desert was a barren stretch of sand and sagebrush that included the city of Las Vegas. Many creatures found the one-hundred-degree temperature of what some would consider a wasteland quite comfortable. Somehow, they found refuge under the scorching sun. For Frank Carter, the desert creatures were of two variations, those that crawled and those that slithered. Frank believed that very few humans called the desert outside the city their home. In the police lieutenant's eyes, those who did find comfort in the desert's bareness were either mentally disturbed or dead.

The Las Vegas heat always made Frank uncomfortable. He hated the weather in Las Vegas, but he hated the desert outside of it more. Unfortunately, that was where he had to be now. The dead body had been found by a man who was hiking through the barren area just outside the city. The victim had been shot in the face multiple times, and his body had been beaten severely. His arms were tied behind his back, and his feet were bound together at his ankles with blue nylon rope. There wasn't any evidence around or on the body. The only interesting thing about the man was the countless tattoos that seemed to cover him. When the evidence technicians finished taking their photographs, Frank bent down closer to the body to get a better look at the man's decorative ink. He then picked up a blue nylon single length of rope that was lying next to the victim.

What was this used for? Frank asked himself as he examined the long length of rope.

"Lieutenant!" an officer yelled from the bottom of a nearby ditch.

"Yeah, what is it?" Frank asked after standing and looking off in the direction of the officer.

"It looks like we got another body down here."

Frank walked toward the other officer and stood next to him. Down in the ditch was a second body. Frank examined the blue nylon rope in his hand once more. Now, he knew what it had been used for. The second victim was lying on his side, looking up toward the top of the ditch. Like the first man, he was naked and bound at the hands, but not the ankles. Frank signaled for the crime scene technicians to come to his location to process the second victim. He then started down the slight hill toward the second body, and when he got close to it, he made a startling discovery.

"Something wrong?" one of the technicians asked when he caught up to the lieutenant.

"No, process the scene. I'll be down after I make a phone call to the commander. I gotta let him know we have a second victim," Frank explained and hurried back to his car. He started it, turned the air conditioner on high, and made a call.

"What is it?" Leontii asked.

"I found your men," Frank answered and then paused. "I got two naked bodies in the desert. I didn't recognize the first one. He was shot multiple times in the face and was beaten severely. When we found the second one, I recognized him. It was Sava."

"Who did it?"

"I don't know. You probably have a better guess than I do," Frank answered sarcastically and ended the call when he unexpectedly saw his commander arriving on the scene.

Leontii sat in front of his desk, thinking about what the police lieutenant had said.

"Shot, beaten, and naked. Hmm," he said under his breath.

Rodeo Drive was crowded with shoppers dressed in their thousand-dollar, designer-label outfits and matching shoes. Morgan dragged an uncomfortable Chance Hardway into the pretentious clothing stores and jewelry shops, where she browsed the racks and counters. The two had been shopping and walking around the different tourist spots in and around Los Angeles all morning, and now part of the afternoon.

Chance was tired of shopping, but he wasn't going to say anything, nor was he going to rush Morgan along. Today, she seemed to be happy and at peace, and he wasn't going to do anything to change that. Instead, he took a seat on a bench inside a designer handbag store and gave Morgan the freedom to peruse the counters and shelves.

"May I help you, sir?" the salesman asked in a snooty tone.

Chance looked up at the man standing in front of him. The man was wearing blue-and-white pinstripe pajamas with brown leather dress shoes.

Chance shook his head. "Nah, I'm okay," he answered and looked at Morgan, who was staring at him and clearly wondering what was going on.

"Well, we don't allow people to loiter in the store."

"I'm not loitering. I need some pajamas. Where can I find some like yours?" Chance asked.

The store associate's face twisted. "Hmph, this is not a pajama set! It is a suit, sir."

"Oh, well, never mind. I don't need a suit," Chance replied.

Two security guards walked over and stood on opposite sides of the bench. The men wore black suits and tried to appear intimidating. Chance stood and looked at the two of them.

Knowing what was about to transpire, Morgan rushed over and took Chance by the arm, then pulled him toward the door.

"Looks like I was leaving anyway," Chance stated and turned toward Morgan.

"Yeah, you better!" one of the security men blurted and pushed Chance in the back.

"Why did you have to do that?" Morgan asked the security guard rhetorically.

"What? Look at this guy! What are you doing, slumming?" the other guard asked as he reached out, about to put his hand on Chance's shoulder.

Chance took the man's hand and turned it to the inside, then bent it backward, causing the man to drop to his knees in pain. The second security officer took a step forward toward Chance.

"Come any closer, and you can join him on the floor," Chance warned, stopping the other man cold. "I think an apology is in order." Chance looked down at the man he held down with his hand.

"I'm sorry. I'm sorry."

"Thank you," Morgan replied. "By the way, I won't be giving you five stars when I rate my shopping experience later today." She pulled Chance out the door.

Frank stood at the back of the coroner's van after the second body was loaded inside. He looked over and saw the news media had gathered nearby, waiting for the police lieutenant to give them a statement. Frank was not only the staff officer who oversaw the investigation of the two homicides, but he was also one of the department's public information officers. Before facing the media, Frank called his people over.

"We only have the one body the media knows about. We are keeping the second on the down-low for now. Do I make myself clear?" Frank asked in a straightforward and authoritative tone. He then turned away from the group and walked to the news crews to give a statement.

Mr. Edward Romano Sr. made it to Kansas City, Missouri, by seven o'clock. His men promptly checked everyone into the hotel once they arrived. The hotel was on Baltimore Avenue in the downtown area. It was older and expensive, but Mr. Romano expected nothing less than the best. After checking in, Mr. Romano and his men walked across the street to the Italian restaurant. Usually, the leader of the Romano crime family never ventured too far out of Philadelphia, but the current situation required the sixty-something Mafia boss to do just that.

The Favolosa Italian Ristorante was a traditional Italian-themed restaurant that served costly meals. Mr. Romano took a seat at the end of the table. He kept his back to the wall while two of his captains filled the seats to the right and left of him. Four other men sat at tables close by. He then had two more men standing outside on the sidewalk, who tried to look inconspicuous by walking up and down the sidewalk in front of the restaurant. When the waitress came by, the boss ordered wine for everyone at his table. He decided to wait to order food until after the meeting.

When the wine came, Mr. Romano took a sip just as one of his men signaled from the window. The others were on their way inside. The boss placed his wine glass on the table and stood when Leontii Adamovich walked into the establishment, followed closely by his Bratva entourage.

Leontii walked to the table, stood next to Edward Romano, and offered his hand. The Philly crime boss reciprocated the gesture, and the two men shook hands. Leontii looked at his men and nodded, a signal for them to be seated. Leontii took the seat at the other end of the table directly across from Edward Romano Sr.

"Thank you for taking my meeting," Leontii stated, opening the dialogue.

"You're welcome. Now, what can I do for you?" Romano asked and drank more wine.

"An associate of mine was killed in Philadelphia, and it is my understanding that your men were there. I would like to know why he was killed and who ordered it." Leontii took a drink of the wine that the waitress had placed in front of him.

"Your comment seems to suggest I know who did it or may have arranged it. Sadly, I don't know why your associate was killed, but I know who did it," Mr. Romano explained.

"Will you tell me?" Leontii asked.

"Yes, for a price."

Chance and Morgan ate an early dinner in Los Angeles and enjoyed an evening drive back to Sin City. They made it back shortly before nine o'clock. The two of them showered, cuddled next to each other in bed, and turned on the evening news.

"In local news, a man's body was found in a desolate area of the desert outside of Las Vegas."

Chance and Morgan watched and listened to the news anchor as she explained the only details currently available regarding the investigation. They were surprised to see someone they were familiar with giving a statement.

"Are you kidding me!" Morgan commented when she saw Lieutenant Frank Carter on the screen.

"A man's body was found by a hiker earlier today, and Las Vegas Metro is investigating the circumstances surrounding the man's death. All possibilities surrounding this suspicious death are being explored, and we should know more later," Frank stated and then walked away from the cameras and the reporters who were still asking him questions.

Morgan looked at Chance and shook her head. She was angry that Frank Carter was still a member of Metro and not rotting in prison somewhere.

"How does a man like that get away with it?" she asked.

"I don't know. Maybe it's because he's a slimy snake who slithers his way out of everything," Chance suggested, then turned the TV off and kissed her.

"What's on your mind?" Morgan asked as she moved over on top of him.

"The same thing that's on yours, baby."

Leontii walked back onto the private jet and sat in the leather seat. The trip to Kansas City had been informative. He knew the Romano family didn't kill his man, but they knew who did. They were willing to tell him who it was, but first, they wanted something from the Bratva.

The other men of the Bratva took their seats, and the jet taxied down the runway. Igor sat next to Leontii but didn't say anything. He knew the brigadier had a lot on his mind, just like others within the Bratva. The entire criminal organization's echelon wondered where their money was and how they would get to it. Normally, Ivan would have had access to it but Anton never sent him the new bank accounts or the passwords before he died.

"Igor, please get me a drink," Leontii told his bodyguard as he took out his cell phone and called Frank Carter.

"Yeah."

"I need you to do something," Leontii stated and took the drink from Igor.

"What is it?"

"I need some wet work done," Leontii answered flatly.

"How wet?" Frank asked after a brief moment.

"An ocean of it."

Frank thought for a moment once again before answering. He needed to calculate what an ocean was worth.

"How wet could I or will I get?" Frank asked. He needed to know what his exposure would be.

"Extremely, and you'll need some people with skills, the kind of skills your country's highly trained military operators have."

"I'm not saying yes until we meet and discuss it, but I'm interested."

"Fine. Call your men now and have them get ready. This needs to be done soon." Leontii ended the phone call. He sat looking out the cabin window at the Kansas City lights that disappeared as the jet gained altitude.

"Why don't we do this ourselves?" Igor asked.

"We can't have this coming back on us. Lieutenant Carter has the connections that are needed to pull this off. This could get very messy," Leontii confessed and turned back toward the window. Whatever Carter was going to charge for the job, it was going to be worth it. The Gorky family needed the man's name who they now suspected possessed the thumb drive with their account numbers, the passwords, and the location of their money. Right now, there were millions of dollars on the line.

CHAPTER 4
VLADIMIR DUDKO

On October 8, 1871 at approximately 9:00 p.m., it was rumored that Mrs. O'Leary's favorite cow, Daisy, kicked over a lantern, igniting the Great Chicago Fire. The fire burned over three square miles of the city, killing nearly three hundred people and making tens of thousands of people homeless. Ever since that unforgettable fire, the neighborhood has been built and rebuilt many times over. Now, at the corner of Taylor and Clinton, very close to where the notorious fire started nearly 150 years ago, sits the Chicago Fire Department's Survive Alive House.

At five o'clock, Aileen McLaughlin, a Chicago fire arson investigator, left the Survive Alive House's business offices after her business meeting. Usually, Aileen would have headed home, but not on this particular afternoon. Instead of walking to her car parked across the street, Aileen walked east on Taylor. She then turned right on Clinton toward the prearranged meeting location. The sidewalks were crowded with Chicagoans. They were either going home or going to dinner at one of the many restaurants lining Clinton.

For the last fifteen years, Aileen had been a dedicated

investigator for the city of Chicago. Over those fifteen years, Investigator McLaughlin had investigated countless suspicious fires and arrested hundreds of arsonists. She had never crossed any line that would jeopardize her career, her integrity, or her morals—until yesterday anyway. One year ago, Aileen fell in love with Patrick. Two months ago, she married Patrick, and just yesterday, she agreed to help get Patrick out of the family business.

Like Aileen, Patrick was of Irish descent, and they both had long ancestral ties within the Irish community of Chicago. Aileen's family had been working within the Chicago Fire Department and the Chicago Police Department as far back as 1860. Unfortunately, Patrick's family's ancestral history was not so heavily involved in public service. Patrick's family history also dated back to 1860, but there were no police officers and no firefighters, only the Irish Mafia.

Three months before the newlyweds were married, Patrick's brother, Brady McLaughlin, was arrested and charged with arson and murder. The younger McLaughlin brother was accused of setting fire to a warehouse that killed a night watchman. Investigator McLaughlin was not allowed to investigate the fire due to her relationship with the accused's brother. However, she did have access to the evidence room that held the video of him setting the fire.

One month before the wedding, Aileen was approached by Michael, the patriarch of the McLaughlin family. He asked her to get the video of his son setting the fire and bring it to him, and in return, she and Patrick would receive a very generous wedding gift. The gift was an 1896 gray stone inline home on North Astor Street that cost well over what she and Patrick could have afforded on their combined salaries. Patrick could have qualified for the house by himself, but as an employee for the McLaughlin crime family, not all his income was accounted for on his taxes.

As Aileen turned east on Roosevelt, she thought about how she could have ever gotten involved with someone like Patrick. She was a college graduate, a former firefighter, and street smart. Like the rest of her family, she knew who the McLaughlin family was and how they earned their livelihood, but still, she couldn't resist Patrick's wit, charm, and good looks.

The gray stone on the North Astor home was beautiful, and anyone would have been overjoyed to receive such a wedding gift. Still, Aileen wanted more. She wanted Patrick's release. If Michael McLaughlin wanted the video of his favorite son committing a murder, he had to agree to allow Patrick to be released from criminal activity. She wanted Patrick to have the opportunity to put his law degree to work and earn a legal income. Michael McLaughlin agreed to it yesterday, if Aileen got him the video.

Michael McLaughlin had somehow gotten a copy of the warehouse's video the night before the fire. He'd had it manipulated and then handed it to Aileen two days ago. Aileen simply had to replace one video thumb drive for another, which she did, earlier this morning. Now she was to meet with her father-in-law and Patrick for dinner.

"Hug, handshake, and pass it off. Hug, handshake, and pass it off. Hug, handshake, and pass it off," Aileen whispered to herself over and over as she got closer to the restaurant. It was a hand-to-hand technique Patrick had told her about and then practiced with her countless times in their living room last night.

Aileen reached Kelly's, a traditional Irish bar and restaurant, at a little past the half hour. She opened the large brown wooden door, walked inside, and quickly found Patrick and Michael sitting at a table in the back. When Aileen reached them, both men stood and greeted her. Patrick hugged his wife, kissed her lips, and gave her a reassuring smile. Michael reached out with both arms and hugged his daughter-in-law.

He then released her and held both Aileen's tiny hands in his callused, baseball-mitt sized hands and kissed her cheek. Aileen did precisely as she and Patrick had practiced. The transfer was quick and without a mistake.

Aileen felt as if an enormous burden had been lifted from her life once the thumb drive left her hand and was no longer in her possession. She took a seat next to her husband, who was seated directly across the table from her father-in-law.

"I believe Patrick has some good news to share," the Mafia boss stated as he nodded in the direction of his son.

"Really, what?" Aileen asked nervously.

"The moving company is scheduled to start moving our stuff out of our apartment in the morning and deliver it to our new house. On North Astor Street," Patrick said, surprising her.

"What? I thought we had another month before we could close on it?" Aileen asked excitedly as she looked back and forth between the two McLaughlin men.

"Actually, I purchased the home a day after the wedding," Michael answered.

"But you didn't know if I would—"

"Didn't know if I knew that you were the right woman for my son? Trust me, I knew. The house isn't the only good news my son has for you this evening."

"What?" Aileen asked and turned and looked at her husband.

"I got a job."

"Where?" Aileen asked enthusiastically.

"The Law Firm of Murphy, Ryan, and Walsh."

"That's great news," Aileen replied with a lot less enthusiasm in her voice than before. She knew of the prestigious law firm that practiced in The Windy City. She also knew they represented every member of the McLaughlin crime family. The heavy burden returned.

It was Chance's first time in Chicago, and thus far, the information Freddy had provided was accurate. Aileen McLaughlin, an attractive brunette, left the Chicago Fire Department's Survive Alive House at five o'clock. That was when Chance started following her. Chance stayed far enough behind that she wouldn't notice him. As he did so, he pondered how a woman who appeared to be a successful fire investigator could have fallen in love with someone deep inside the Irish Mafia.

Kelly's Bar had hardwood floors and Celtic-themed decorations covering the walls. A horseshoe-shaped bar sat at the restaurant's east side, where a green light illuminated the custom carved bar top. Various Irish beers and other spirits lined the wall behind it, and the bar itself was white granite with gray streaks running through it. From at the end of the bar, Chance watched Aileen and the two men she had joined as they ordered their drinks and dinner.

Chance observed Aileen nervously hand the thumb drive off to the older man when they greeted each other. The thumb drive is what Chance had come to get. He didn't know what was on it, nor did he care. Freddy wanted it, which usually meant someone else wanted it and was willing to pay to get it. Therefore, Chance had to get it. Getting it was all that mattered to Chance if he wanted Freddy's information on the fourth Russian's location.

Chance ordered a soda and looked around at everyone inside the restaurant. Everyone seemed to be enjoying their dinner and drinks, except the two men who sat close to Aileen and the two other men at their table. The two other men closely watched every person who walked to the table or by it.

Two bodyguards that I can see and possibly one more somewhere. There's always the plus-one rule. Every cop is taught the rule in the academy. Wherever there are bad guys, there's usually one more somewhere, Chance thought as he continued to survey his surroundings but didn't see anyone else to be concerned about.

Chance was trying to decide how to get his hands on the thumb drive when the older man unexpectedly got up from the table and walked toward the bathroom with the two bodyguards close behind. Chance took the opportunity and followed the three men. When he entered the bathroom, he found one bodyguard standing next to the door.

"It's a bit crowded in here. You may want to wait a minute," Liam advised the man who walked into the bathroom behind him. Liam was Michael McLaughlin's number one man and had been for ten years. On two occasions, Liam had been shot protecting the notorious Irish Mafia boss.

"It's all right. I gotta go, and a minute could be a minute too long," Chance stated as he brushed by the man. He looked around the bathroom and saw there were two stalls and three urinals. Michael McLaughlin stood in front of the urinal on the far left. His bodyguard stood in front of the urinal on the far right.

At least they practice proper male bathroom etiquette, Chance thought to himself as he took his place in front of the middle urinal. He looked over at the bodyguard on his right and smiled.

Conner was a young Irishman and was on his first job with the McLaughlin family. The man standing next to him, and his smile, made the young man feel uncomfortable.

Chance could see he was making the young man uneasy, so he made his move. As he continued to smile at the young man, he looked down.

"You're pissing on your shoes," Chance stated and then looked back up at the bodyguard.

"What?" Conner asked and looked down. Chance took the opportunity he had created and threw a hard elbow in Conner's jaw, knocking him out. He then quickly turned and slammed the crime boss's head into the wall.

Michael McLaughlin was stunned. He dropped to his knees while his attacker turned toward Liam. Liam reached into his coat, pulled out his revolver, and pointed it at the man who had attacked them.

Chance saw the gun coming out and moved forward, spinning into the bodyguard while grabbing his gun hand. He used his right elbow and delivered five quick strikes to the man, knocking him out. He then walked back to the crime boss and lifted him off the floor.

"You'll regret this," Michael warned.

"Probably, but I need what's in your pocket," Chance explained as he reached into the man's coat, took out the thumb drive, and put it into his own pocket. He dropped the man back onto the floor, then walked out of the bathroom and out of the restaurant.

Chance placed the thumb drive into an already-addressed envelope, took a picture of it, dropped it into a mailbox, and drove away. He called Freddy to tell him it was done, and Freddy sent him the address of the fourth Russian.

Vladimir Dudko was settling in for the evening. He had just gotten back into town from Russia and his meeting with the Gorky family. It was decided that Vlad would be responsible for promoting someone from his local Bratva to replace Anton. The family needed someone who knew how to work the books, find their money, and get it back now that Anton had been killed. The entire Bratva was busy trying to find their money and the man responsible for killing Anton.

Vlad walked around his kitchen, preparing himself and his best friend, Maxim, a late-night dinner. He had a few men sitting outside, guarding the house. The Gorky family had decided they couldn't take any chances on anyone else in the organization getting killed. Maxim had gone on the trip to Russia as well. He was a soldier who controlled the shipments of women who were brought into the country to work. On the plane back to Chicago, the two men decided to spend the evening with some women in their employment. Now, they were waiting for the women to arrive.

"Vlad! Vlad! Where's the food?" Maxim yelled from the living room.

Vlad hurried into the room. "I'm coming, comrade."

"You're a superb host, but I should be making your food. You're the boss; I am not."

Vlad grinned. "Yes, but tonight, you're my houseguest." He declared and placed the tray on the coffee table just as the doorbell rang.

"I'll get that," Maxim said as he removed his cloth napkin from his lap. He walked to the front door and opened it.

Chance found Vladimir Dudko's home easily. He parked down the road, walked up to the corner of the property, and surveyed the outside. The house was dark. There were no driveway lights, no house lights, and nothing else to indicate anyone was home. Still, Chance approached the house carefully. When he got to the front door, he found it open. Slowly, he walked inside, and lying on the floor was a man who appeared to have been shot.

Chance continued into the house and found two more dead men piled on top of each other in the hallway. He walked into the living room where he found the man he was looking for. Lying over a tray of freshly prepared food was Vladimir Dudko. He, too, appeared to have been shot multiple times. Chance quickly turned around to walk out of the house. When he got to the front door, however, he paused. The man lying next to the door was moving. Maxim propped himself up and looked up at the unfamiliar man.

"Who are you?" Maxim asked in a low, raspy voice.

"No one," Chance answered as he knelt next to the Russian. He reached over and grabbed a cloth towel lying next to the man and placed it over his injured shoulder. Chance then took the man's hand and lifted it to his wound.

"Apply pressure," Chance instructed. He reached into the man's pocket, found his cell phone, and handed it to him. He then stood and walked out of the house. He got into the rental car and drove away.

Maxim lay on the floor, bleeding. He closed his eyes for a moment, took a deep breath, and dialed the number.

"Hello," the man on the other end answered in Russian.

"I need a cleanup service and a veterinarian," Maxim stated.

"Where?"

Maxim had called the number that he and everyone in the Bratva would call in a situation like this. After he gave Vlad's address to the cleanup crew, he put the phone down and waited. As Maxim lay there, he thought about the man he had just met and wondered who he was, why he was here, and what the man would do next. Vlad was in pain, but he knew he would survive. The only thing he needed more than a doctor was the identity of the man who just walked out.

While waiting for his flight, Chance called Morgan. He desperately wanted to be with her back in Las Vegas. He waited for her to answer but the call went to her voicemail. Chance left her a quick message. He then sat there and thought about what he had walked in on at Vladimir Dudko's home.

When Morgan stepped out of the shower, she stood in front of the mirror and looked at her face. The plastic surgeon had done an excellent job covering the scars, but Morgan could still make out the faint marks of where they were along her cheeks. She ran her finger down the light-pink line that was followed by a single tear. She then dried her eyes, picked up her cell phone to turn on some music, and noticed the missed call and a message from Chance. She walked into the bedroom and sat on the edge of the bed to play the message.

"Hey, baby, it's me. I'm about to get on the plane to come home. I just wanted to let the most beautiful girl in the world know I was thinking about her and that I couldn't wait to see her. I'll be there in a few hours. I love you, see you soon."

Morgan replayed the message over and over. She smiled each time. "He loves me."

CHAPTER 5
AN OCEAN OF WATER

It was nine o'clock in the morning. The sun was already sitting in the eastern sky over the Nevada desert. Leontii had been in his office at the Emerald Coast Casino since after midnight. From his office window, Leontii had been watching the sunrise since the early morning hours. The hooker sleeping on the sofa was nothing more than a distraction that Leontii needed after getting the call from Chicago. Now, he waited for another call. All he knew was that Vladimir Dudko was dead, along with his guards, and that Maxim Orlov was the only one who had survived, and he had been in surgery all morning.

"Do you want to go again?" Lesley asked after she awoke and saw the Russian standing half-dressed in front of the window.

"No, you can get dressed and leave," Leontii answered

Frank Carter was sitting in his office, reading over the coroner's report regarding the two homicides in the desert, when his cell phone rang. He was expecting two phone calls this morning, and this one was the first.

"It's about time," Frank growled when he answered the call.

"I've been busy," Ricky Gallup replied.

"Are you spending all of our money?" Frank asked. He was concerned that Ricky was reckless with the money he had taken from the Hermanos Nation, the money that Frank believed belonged to him as well.

"No, I got most of 'my' money left. I only took five hundred thousand. The rest is still sitting in the storage unit I rented. We're still short half the money we need to pay back your people and to buy another shipment." Ricky explained, making sure to let Frank know that the money was his as he did so.

"That's why I need your help."

"What kind of help?" Ricky asked.

"The hazardous kind."

"If I'm apprehended, what kind of sentence am I looking at?"

"The death penalty kind," Frank answered.

"How much is the employer willing to pay for it?"

"I'm asking for seven figures."

"Will it be enough for us to finish with what you owe and to get more product?"

"Yeah," Frank quickly answered.

"Let's meet tonight and discuss it."

"Okay. I'll call you later and tell you where to meet me. I gotta get more information anyway," Frank said and ended the call. A few seconds later, the second call came in.

"Yeah," Frank said when he answered the call. He listened for a moment. "I'll text you the address."

The woods were quiet, and no one ever came to the cabin, except for federal agents. The log cabin sat right on Lake Tahoe. It was once a retreat for some financial wizard who had made millions embezzling the rich and famous, until he got caught and was convicted by the federal government. The government seized his assets, which included the cabin. Now, the US Marshal Service used the multimillion-dollar cabin as a place to hide their witnesses, witnesses like Henry Willard.

Henry sat in his room watching TV, just as he did every day unless he was swimming in the heated pool or playing video games. He grew tired of being in protective custody three months ago, but there seemed to be light at the end of the tunnel. His handler, Marshal Jessica Wheeler, had told him that Junior, the man he saw with the gun that night, shooting at people, was being extradited to Las Vegas to stand trial. When the feds first approached Henry about testifying, he refused to do it because he was afraid of retaliation from the Romano family, but when he was told the federal government would set him up in another state under a new identity, along with a monthly allowance, Henry took the deal. He had no family, no real job to speak of, and no girlfriend—until he fell in love with Jessica Wheeler, which was something the two of them kept secret.

"What are you doing, Henry?" Marshal Dillon Wilson asked. Wilson was one of the four men who worked the day shift protecting Henry. The day shift was a little laxer than the night shift, and on occasions, they even played poker with their star witness.

"Nothing, as usual," Henry answered somberly.

"It could be over pretty soon. Have you looked at the list of names we gave you? I mean, it's only a matter of time before the 'new you' will be born."

"Yeah, but who chooses those names? C'mon, who wants to be a Dillon?" Henry asked rhetorically and laughed.

"Yeah, I get it. Who'd want that name?" Dillon asked and then laughed along with his witness.

The jail cell had concrete walls that were painted a dull beige. There was a sink, a toilet, and a metal bed frame fastened to the wall. Junior lay there on top of the thin mattress, waiting to be taken back to Las Vegas. The jail he was being held in was somewhere in Illinois, but Junior didn't know where. The state police had handed him off to the feds, and they put him in an armored car with no windows. The people who brought him his food didn't wear a uniform, there wasn't anything in the jail cell that would hint at his location, and he wasn't allowed to have visitors.

"Let's go," a man ordered.

Junior looked up and saw the US Marshal and another man standing in front of the cell door, unlocking it.

"Where're we going?" Junior asked as he stood and walked to the bars.

"Back to Vegas," the Marshal answered and entered the cell with the prisoner.

"Now?" Junior asked.

"Yes." The other man put handcuffs on the prisoner. He placed a hood over his head and escorted him out of the cell.

"This is bullshit!" Junior protested as he was led out to the parking lot.

An army of US Marshals waited to escort the prisoner to the waiting jet.

Chance's flight left Chicago at six in the morning. He fell asleep before the plane took off, and he didn't wake up until it landed in Las Vegas. As the plane taxied down the runaway, Chance thought about the previous evening. He had so many questions.

Who killed Vladimir? Why was he killed? Why was he killed

on the night that I was going to be there? Was it a coincidence?
Chance asked himself.

He was still running the same questions over and over in his
mind when they started deplaning at the gate. He grabbed his
bag from the overhead and slowly made his way off the plane,
through the terminal, and out to the curb where he found a
beautiful woman waiting for him in a custom-built Ford F100.

"Come here often?" Morgan joked.

"Would you like me to drive?" Chance asked after opening
the passenger door.

"No, I rather enjoy driving this old hotrod of yours. Get
in," Morgan ordered.

Chance got in the truck, pulled her close, and kissed her
like she had never been kissed before. Morgan loved the way
Chance was with her. He was a possessive, passionate, and
every bit of a man, but the best thing about him was that he
was her man.

Leontii disliked meeting in locations that were in the slums,
but this was where Frank Carter had decided they should meet.
A storage building wasn't what the Russian had had in mind
when he told Frank earlier to choose a meeting spot, but here
he was. The Brigadier got out of the car and followed Igor
toward the building, past the crime scene tape, and into a small
office in the back.

"This is an interesting place," Leontii announced as he
entered the office.

Frank was sitting behind the desk and looked up at his
guest.

"Did you decorate it yourself?" the Russian asked as he
took a seat across from the corrupt police lieutenant.

"It's as good as any other. Besides, I have control over it.
Now, what do you want me to do?" Frank asked flatly. He

wasn't in the mood for games or listening to any smartass comments. He wanted to know what the job was.

"Very well. The US Marshals are bringing this man to Las Vegas early in the morning, and I need you to intervene with his arrival," Leontii explained and handed over a photo. Frank looked at the man in the picture and recognized him right away. He looked back up at Leontii.

"This specific man will be costly," Frank stated.

"I thought so. How much?"

"Nine million," the lieutenant stated without hesitating.

"Why so much?" Leontii asked, already knowing the answer.

"Because people are going to die. People like US Marshals, local cops, and civilians. My exposure will be well beyond anything I could have imagined. This is a deep ocean of wet work."

"Fine, but you must run this on your own, and you and you only will be responsible. If you fail, then that failure will fall on you," Leontii warned.

"That sounds like a threat."

"No, it's not a threat; it's a promise. If you're having trouble understanding the difference between the two, allow me to clarify. If you fuck this up, I will kill you!"

"Who do you think—"

"I think," the Russian said, interrupting Frank. "I'm the man who owns your corrupt ass."

Frank stood. "No one owns me!"

"I think you're mistaken about that," Leontii said proudly as King James walked into the office with two of his men.

Frank got nervous and was unsure about what to say or do. He owed Edward "King" James seven million dollars. He sat back down and looked around the room.

"So, no one owns you. Is that what I heard you say?" Edward asked. King James was a Los Angeles crime boss who was a notable hard money lender. James had made his fortune during the early 80s selling crack cocaine when it first hit the streets. He had been in and out of prison more times than he could remember. If he had a resume, it would read "career criminal" as his profession. King James had financed the purchase of Frank's heroin months ago. He had expected to make twenty percent off his investment, which went up in flames in the same building he was now standing in.

"Yes, that's exactly what I said. Neither of you two fucks own me!" Frank declared as he stood up again and walked toward King James. He decided he wouldn't be pushed around by some street thug and an uneducated Russian mobster. Besides, he figured they needed him.

"Just a minute!" James ordered as one of his bodyguards moved in front of him and reached for his gun.

Frank pulled his own gun and shot the bodyguard in the foot. The man dropped to the floor as Frank grabbed the second man, forced him down onto his knees, and placed his gun to the man's head.

"I know I owe you money, and I'm working on getting you paid back. Don't ever come at me again. I'll fucking kill you and your entire crew," Frank declared and released the second man.

"Then pay me back!" King James demanded.

"Fine. I owe you eight point four million after you add on the twenty percent. That debt is now his after I do the job he wants me to do." Frank pointed at Leontii.

"Agreed," Leontii replied and looked at King James.

"Okay, but I better get my money. Russian Mafia or not, I will get what's mine one way or another," King James declared. He turned around and walked out of the room with his beaten men.

It was after midnight when Chance got out of bed and walked into the living room. He was quiet and made sure not to wake Morgan. He had been awake since the two of them had gone to bed earlier. He had lain there staring at the ceiling, trying to figure out what was going on with the Russians.

"Something's not right," he whispered as he sat on the couch and replayed the events in Philly and Chicago. He couldn't put his finger on it, but he knew something was wrong. He looked over and picked up the two thumb drives he had taken from Anton. They had been sitting in a glass dish ever since he got back from Philadelphia. "I need to see what's on these too."

"On what?" a sleepy Morgan asked from the doorway.

"Nothing," Chance answered as he looked up and saw her standing there in nothing but one of his T-shirts. He dropped the thumb drives back in the dish, walked toward her, placed his arms around her waist, and walked her back to bed.

Frank had returned to his office by nine o'clock, and Ricky Gallup arrived at ten. The police lieutenant had been working on a plan for the new job. Before Leontii left the previous evening, he handed over a file with the information he had gathered about the man in the photo.

Ricky took a seat on the other side of the desk and waited for Frank to finish what he was doing. Frank wrote notes on a sheet of paper he had sitting on top of a Las Vegas map. The map covered most of the desk, and when he was finished, he looked at Ricky.

"I guess all of this is part of the job that we gotta do," Ricky stated as he stood and looked over the map.

"Yeah. Do you have anyone we can call for help on this?" Frank asked.

"Run everything by me first."

"All right," Frank agreed and handed over the target's photo before he explained the job.

Chance and Morgan had slept in until about ten o'clock. After they got dressed, they decided to drive out to Henderson to have lunch at a local Mexican restaurant. Chance enjoyed fajitas, while Morgan ate two steak tacos. He sat with his back to the wall, where he viewed everyone coming into the establishment. He, like most cops and military operators, never sat with his back to the door.

Morgan didn't mind sitting with her back to the door. It allowed her to avoid seeing or being seen by someone she knew. The two were having a pleasant conversation when Chance saw a familiar face walk by the front window.

"What's she doing in Henderson?" Chance asked.

"Who?" Morgan turned around to look in the same direction as Chance.

"Rebecca Hicks. I just watched her go by. She looked in the window and saw me but quickly looked away as if she didn't see me."

"Who?"

"She's someone I had business with. Wait here," Chance stated before getting up and walking to the front door, where he looked out the glass toward the parking lot. Toward the back, he saw Rebecca standing next to a black sedan with tinted windows. She was speaking to someone inside the car, but he couldn't see who it was. He then watched her walk over to her car, get in, and drive away while the sedan stayed in the parking lot.

"Let's go," Chance ordered after walking back to the table. He held a hundred-dollar bill in the air at their server, dropped it on the table, and rushed Morgan out the door toward his truck.

"What's going on?" Morgan asked frantically as she looked around.

"I don't know, but I don't like it," Chance answered as he hurried out of the parking lot while keeping an eye on the sedan that pulled out behind him.

Chance and Morgan made it home late in the afternoon after losing the tail that had followed them out of the parking lot in Henderson. Once they arrived back in Las Vegas, Chance drove into a casino's parking garage and searched his truck. He discovered a tracking device that had been placed under it. He attached it to another car with California plates that was parked next to him. Chance and Morgan got back to his place around three o'clock.

At five o'clock Morgan made the two of them a small snack, and while Chance was relaxing on his couch, he received a text message from Freddy with one name listed in the message. *Vasily Zlobin*. Vasily was one of the other men on his hit list.

It was dangerous for him to leave Las Vegas so soon after discovering someone was tailing him. However, he still had anger deep inside that drove him to seek out the men who had hurt the woman he loved. After Morgan went to bed, he responded to the text.

"Send me the information."

"I think we'll need about four more guys, all of whom will need heavy body armor, fully automatic AR-15s, 9 millimeters, flashbangs, and some high explosives," Ricky stated and fell back into the chair. The two men had spent most of the day coming up with a plan.

"Only four? I mean, there are three SUVs, one lead car, and one tail car, not to mention the overwatch units at the various intersections."

"Yeah, four is good. Plus you and I make a total of six. I

mean, you are helping, right?" Ricky asked in a tone that told Frank it was more of an expectation than a suggestion.

"Yeah, I'm in on this one," Frank replied.

"Okay, I'll call some guys and have them here by tonight. It'll cost us about a hundred and fifty grand for each man for this kind of job."

"We can cover it for now, and then after we get paid, we can replace it. Then we'll get on with our own private business," Frank explained and sat down.

"Okay, but don't forget that we're seventy-thirty in our private deal."

"I remember," Frank mumbled.

"Good, make sure you don't forget. I could've taken all the money and killed you that night," Ricky said, reminding Frank about the night the police lieutenant had brought El Toro and his men to Ricky's hotel room to kill him.

"I got it!" Frank replied angrily. He figured after the nine million the Russians were paying him for the job, he had six hundred thousand left after King James was made whole to pay for the other operators. Frank also had one million of his own money to add to the money Ricky still had. Then, after they bought nearly seven million worth of heroin, they would make about seven more from cutting it up and selling it, which he got thirty percent of after their expenses. Frank expected to make close to six million, maybe more, if he could figure out a way to kill Ricky when they were done.

CHAPTER 6
VASILY ZLOBIN

The Los Angeles skyline with the Pacific Ocean's deep blue water in the background was a spectacular view from the deck of Tommy Black's beach house. Tommy was a high-profile Hollywood producer who lavished in the wealth that his chosen career had afforded him. He spent Thursday through Saturday partying into the early morning hours at the best nightclubs around Los Angeles. If the A-listers of Hollywood were there, so was Tommy Black. He was one of the biggest producers in showbusiness. Tommy was the type of man who took advantage of people who were desperate to be in the movies, especially women. It was all about power for the five-foot-six, overweight but influential movie producer.

Club New Alphas was the newest and most popular nightspot in the City of Angels, and Tommy's favorite place to prospect. The youngest, most original, and most attractive talent in Los Angeles did anything they could to get in the door of the trendy nightclub. There was always a line of people wrapped around the building every night. Tommy never had to wait in line; why would he? After all, he secretly owned the club—well, half of it anyway.

Tonight was a busy night for New Alphas, and when Tommy arrived, he found the line outside the club a little longer than usual. He smiled as his driver stopped along the curb to let him out of the luxury car. Tommy knew that tonight there would be countless bright-eyed hopefuls willing to do anything to get their big break in Hollywood. In the middle of the line waiting to get into the club, Tommy spotted a particular woman. She was about five foot five and 110 pounds, with blonde hair and a curvy figure. Tommy didn't think she was the next Hollywood movie star, but she did look like the next adult movie star.

The new doorman, Logan, watched over the crowd when he saw Mr. Black walking toward the entrance. He immediately opened the red rope barrier to allow the club owner access to the front of the line.

"Good evening, sir," Logan said, greeting the man.

"Evening. I guess you're the new guy, Logan, right?" Tommy asked.

"Yes, sir, I am. I'm incredibly happy to finally meet you."

"Likewise. Can you do me a favor and have that blonde brought inside and to my private table?" Tommy asked as he pointed toward the woman, who pretended not to notice the well-known and very recognizable movie producer pointing at her.

Logan opened the club door. "Yes, right away."

"Thank you," Tommy said and walked inside, but not before looking at the handsome new doorman again. *I need to get him into a movie,* Tommy thought as he made his way to his private table in the back. Even though Tommy used people for his own personal gain, he had a knack for finding the next big movie star. He thought the new doorman had possibilities.

Logan walked toward the woman standing in line that Mr. Black had pointed out. She smiled when she saw the fit and good-looking doorman approaching her. Tonight, she had her mind set on Tommy Black, the producer, but maybe tomorrow night, she could have the doorman.

"You look like you're looking for someone," the woman flirtatiously suggested as she stepped out of line and brushed her breasts against the man.

"I am, and it looks like I found her," Logan replied.

"I'm Michelle. What can I do for you?" Michelle ran her hand up the doorman's back and onto his shoulders.

"I'm Logan, and Mr. Black would like you to join him at his table."

"I think that would be all right for tonight, but I'm also free tomorrow night," she hinted and then took her hand and rubbed his well-defined biceps before placing her arm under his.

The doorman smiled. "Come this way, please," he replied as he escorted the woman into the club.

New Alphas was crowded with self-centered people dancing as if everyone were there to see them. Other people tried to carry on conversations at small circular tables. At the same time, music blared from speakers in every corner of the nightclub. The DJ spun the newest music on his turntable. He stood on a metal platform that hung from the ceiling over the dance floor. Logan and Michelle moved through the crowd slowly as they made their way toward Tommy Black's private table. After a few minutes, the two stopped at a set of stairs that led up to it.

Michelle turned before she started up the stairs. "Do you think we can see each other tomorrow night?"

"I won't be in town tomorrow night," Logan answered.

She tilted her head. "Leaving so soon?"

Logan nodded. "Yes, going home tonight, actually."

"When?" Michelle questioned suspiciously.

"Just as soon as I take care of some business," Logan answered as he started up the stairs toward the private table.

"What are you talking about?"

"Come with me, and I'll show you," Logan offered as he reached his hand out for hers.

Michelle took Logan's hand and followed him up the stairs. When they reached the top, a bodyguard, Carl, stood there checking people for weapons before they joined Mr. Black. Logan had met Carl before starting his shift and decided he didn't like the tall, burly man.

"What do you want?" Carl asked sarcastically.

"Mr. Black wanted Michelle to join him," Logan answered.

Carl looked at the beautiful women and then back at Tommy Black, who gave his bodyguard the signal to allow the woman to join him.

"All right, you can go on up," Carl stated and allowed Michelle to pass by. "Get your ass back out front, shithead," Carl remarked to Logan as he pointed back toward the club's entrance.

"Yeah, that's not going to happen," Logan replied confidently and started to walk by Carl.

"What the fuck," Carl objected and put his hand on Logan's chest to stop him from walking by.

Logan paused and looked at Carl and then at Tommy, who was wondering what was happening.

"Get back to the fucking door!" Carl ordered and slightly pushed Logan back.

Logan stepped back and made eye contact with Carl before he struck him with a right cross. He followed it up with a hard knee to the surprised man's face, sending him backward onto his back with a busted lip.

"What the hell!" Tommy yelled as he watched Logan walk toward him. "What are you doing, Logan?"

"My name's not Logan, and you are not part owner of this place anymore," Chance replied. He had grown tired of being someone he was not. Besides, he hated the name Logan.

Tommy gave him a dirty look. "What are you talking about?" He asked as he watched the man reach around his back for something.

"No, don't!" Tommy yelled, while Michelle began to cover her eyes.

"Relax, I'm not here to kill you." Chance placed the papers he'd had in his back pocket onto the table in front of the movie producer.

"What?" Tommy asked, surprised.

"You took money from someone for your half of the interest in this place, but you have not signed the paperwork. You must sign over your rights to the club to the new owner," Chance explained as he laid the paperwork out for the man to sign.

Tommy waved his hands and leaned back. "I changed my mind. I don't want to sell."

"I don't care what you want to do or not do. Now sign the papers," Chance ordered.

"Wait—"

Chance grabbed him by the hair and dragged the man to the table and the papers he had placed on it.

"Okay, okay," Tommy said as he signed the documents.

Chance reviewed the signatures and started to walk away with the documents but then stopped. He turned back, looked at the shaken Michelle, and winked at her before he walked down the stairs to leave the club.

Once outside in the parking lot, Chance took a photo of everything, just as he had done with everything else, before dropping it into a mailbox. Finally, he sent the photo to Freddy, who responded back with nothing more than the address Chance needed.

Vasily Zlobin enjoyed his private party, his expensive liquor, and the gorgeous girls he had brought on his yacht. The Malishka cruising yacht was lavishly decorated and was Vasily's pride and joy. The ocean vessel was 180 feet in length, was white with dark-blue trim, and had three levels. The Russian lieutenant had purchased the vessel for twenty million dollars, which was about fifty million less than its actual value. The previous owner needed to settle a debt that had been owed to Vasily. The luxury yacht was practically given as payment, saving the previous owner's life, for a little while anyway.

Vasily, one of the Gorky's lieutenants, as they were commonly referred to within the organization, was known for his one-sided business dealings. He was the type of business partner who made deals and found a way out of them if it benefited him. In Vasily's eyes, every business partnership he was involved in was to be a success. There were no acceptable losses, not for him anyway. If a business owner asked Vasily to invest money with him, it was understood that the business and the business owner could suffer a financial loss but not Vasily. Every month, Vasily wanted his money, and he wanted it on time.

Mila, Nina, and Anya had been brought to the yacht earlier by Oleg, their manager. The term "manager" was used loosely by the Bratva. It meant Oleg was a pimp, a driver, an enforcer, or anything else the girls needed while at work. Usually, the three girls provided services in Los Angeles and the surrounding cities to some of showbusiness's biggest names. All the clients were wealthy, they were screened by the appointment scheduler, and they all paid fifteen hundred dollars for one hour with one of the Bratva's escorts. The girls kept five hundred of those dollars for themselves. The rest went to the Gorky family as repayment for bringing the girls to the United States—and protecting them, of course. The Gorky family allowed the beautiful escorts to keep any additional money they made from upselling their services to clients. On a good night, the three girls saw three to four clients, each of whom made the family anywhere between nine and twelve thousand dollars. One girl could make about four grand a night if she knew how to upsell.

Tonight, the girls would not be traveling around the city entertaining Hollywood elites, nor would the girls make anywhere near four thousand dollars for their services. Since the evening's client was a member of the Bratva, the girls would get a flat fee of one thousand dollars for each of them, but no more. It was an all-inclusive price for all services the girls provided, and it included any and all special requests from the client as well.

Vasily sat on the leather sofa while he intently watched as Mila and Nina danced in front of him. As Mila looked down and smiled, she removed her top, exposing her large breasts to the Bratva lieutenant. Vasily smiled back and looked over at his trusted friend, Pavel Petrov, who was enjoying the very-nude Anya sitting on his lap. Vasily had invited Pavel to join him for the evening. It was not merely because Pavel was Vasily's closest friend that he had been invited. Pavel was the family's number one assassin, and he was particularly good at the art of killing. Vasily figured he was safe with the armed men out on the deck, the ship's crew, and Pavel close by. The Gorky family's order was that all their Bratva take additional protective measures until the man or the men who were killing their people was found and eliminated.

Vasily was growing tired. He wanted to retire to his bedroom and have some fun with Mila and Nina before falling asleep. He drank the rest of his brandy down, took the girls by their hands, and walked toward his bedroom.

"Where are you going, brother?" Pavel asked in his thick Russian accent while slurring his words. The assassin was drunk but wanted the party to continue.

"To bed. I want to fuck before I pass out," Vasily replied and then pulled Mila into him and kissed her breasts.

Pavel drank the rest of his brandy as well. "Fuck. You're too drunk for that. Come sit and drink more. We'll pass out with these beautiful visions in front of us."

"I have this!" Vasily declared as he held up a blue pill. "I'll fuck all night with this."

"Hahaha! With that, you shall be a porno star!" Pavel yelled and then laughed loudly. The laughter got the better of the man. Pavel leaned too far to his left side, which caused both him and Anya to fall from the leather chair onto the floor, where they rolled over each other.

Vasily laughed at the sight of the two of them and then continued toward the bedroom with Mila and Nina in tow.

The crew of the Malishka had worked feverishly to get underway before midnight, and now they were exhausted. Once the ship was out to sea, the captain ordered everyone who wasn't essential to their quarters to get some sleep. Vasily's men worked in shifts, with two men on each deck, and the others were sent to their bunks to sleep until it was time for their shift change in the morning.

Crew member David Johnson was at the back of the yacht checking on the jet skis when his supervisor, William, walked up behind him.

"What are you doing back here?" William asked.

David turned and looked at the older man. "I'm making sure the jet skis are ready for tomorrow."

"Wait a minute, who are you?" William asked suspiciously. He knew every person working in his crew, and the man in front of him was not one of them.

"I'm David," Chance answered and looked at the name tag on his shirt. "David Johnson. See, it says it right here." Chance stepped forward toward William.

"Stop right there!" William ordered and brought his radio up to his mouth.

Chance stepped forward and punched the unsuspecting

William in the face. He fell backward, but Chance grabbed him and gently laid the unconscious man down on the deck. He then looked around to make sure no one had seen them. He dragged the man to the deck rail and laid him next to the two bodyguards, whom he had already knocked out and tied up.

"Now, to find Mr. Zlobin," Chance whispered and made his way to the stairs that led to the center deck.

Vasily was half-dressed and lying on the bed while Mila and Nina enjoyed themselves next to him. He was drunk, tired, and wanting some attention from them.

"Come, please me," he ordered.

Chance made his way through the other two decks, quietly incapacitating the other guards while avoiding the rest of the crew at the same time. He entered the main cabin, where he found a man and woman naked and passed out on the floor. Chance stepped over the two of them and walked down the short hallway to the stateroom in the back. When he got to the door, he paused and listened for a moment. He heard three voices, and when he was about to open the door, he heard someone behind him. Chance spun around quickly, but it was too late. There was a sudden blow to his head and then darkness.

Waves lapped against the shoreline, the morning sun was about to rise, and seagulls could be heard cawing off in the distance. The rubber raft bounced continuously as wave after wave crashed against it, pushing it further and further onto the sandy beach. It was the rolling feeling under his stomach that awakened Chance. He opened his eyes, looked around, and lifted himself up. He rolled over, out of the raft and into the shallow water. He was disoriented and nauseated, and he felt a lump on his head.

What in the hell happened? Chance crawled through the

water toward dry land, leaving the raft to bounce up and down in the surf. He didn't know how long he had been unconscious, but he knew it had to have been a few hours because the sun was rising. As he sat there, he tried to recall the events of the previous evening. Chance remembered sneaking onto the ship before it left the dock. He remembered meeting William by the jet skis. He also recalled each guard he took out. Finally, he remembered walking into the ship's main cabin and finding the couple that was passed out on the floor. The rest of the night was a complete blank.

Chance looked out toward the water and saw the Malishka close to shore. The pain in his head was intense, but he still stood to his feet to get a better look at the yacht anchored a few hundred yards away.

"Why did they let me go? Why did they drop anchor?" Chance whispered just as he witnessed the Malishka explode into a brilliant flash of red and orange flames. The explosion lit the darkness, illuminating the point where the water's surface and the sky met. Chance stood there for a moment before walking away toward what he believed to be the highway behind him.

CHAPTER 7
ROADBLOCKS

The ballgame played on the TV that sat on an old dresser at the foot of the bed. Junior sat on the edge of the bed inside an old rundown hotel on Las Vegas's outskirts. The prisoner's legs and ankles were cuffed. He had one hand free while the other remained chained to his waist. The US Marshals Service had attached two forty-five-pound weights to the chains around his ankles. They weren't taking any chances of the mobster running off or having someone come in and carry him away.

"I need some food!" Junior yelled into the adjoining room.

"We ordered some pizza, Junior. Wait patiently; it'll be here soon!" Marshal Westland yelled back from the other room. Marshal Martin Westland, along with ten other marshals, was assigned to get the young mobster back to Las Vegas for his first appearance in front of Judge Rowland. Marshal Westland was growing sick and tired of listening to Junior complain about anything and everything. The experienced lawman had over twenty-nine years in service to his country, and he was scheduled to retire in three months. He and his wife, Doris, had plans to travel Europe next summer, and that was all he really cared about.

Junior continued. "I'm hungry now."

Martin walked into the room and stood over the young man. "Junior, give me a break. I've been with you nonstop since we picked you up."

"C'mon, Martin, give me a break here."

"Like what kind of break?"

"I gotta use the toilet."

"You know the rules. Three marshals are required to be in here when we remove the restraints. Tom and Dwayne will be back from their smoke break in a few minutes. If you behave, I'll keep the restraints off until it's time to go to bed," Martin said, trying to negotiate with his prisoner.

"You promise?"

"Yes, but behaving means no insulting comments to any of the other guys when they come back inside. Agreed?" Martin asked.

"Okay, I'll agree if you let me have a soda with my pizza and not just water this time."

"Then we have an accord," Martin stated as he reached down and shook the man's free hand.

"That we do." Junior liked Marshal Westland. He, unlike the other marshals, treated him like a human being and not some animal.

Frank reviewed the plan over and over with Ricky. Some of the hired guns had already arrived, and the others were coming in later. Frank left the office during the late afternoon to get the supplies Ricky said they needed. After reviewing the plan, the two men began going through their supplies and dividing them according to each man's responsibility during the hit.

"Is there anything we're forgetting?" Frank asked as he looked around the room at the collection of weapons and explosives.

"No. Have you really thought this through?" Ricky asked.

"What do you mean?"

"It's going to get ugly tomorrow. Federal marshals are going to die, and maybe some of your fellow cops. You might be the one who has to put one of your own men down," Ricky explained as he checked the action on one of the pistols.

"I'll be fine. I've come way too far to allow someone to get in my way, even if it's someone I know," Frank answered without hesitating.

After Chance got back to Las Vegas from Los Angeles, he texted Freddy. *We need to meet.* A few minutes later, Freddy texted back: *Fremont nine o'clock tonight.*

Chance knew that Freddy meant he wanted to meet at his tiny bar on Fremont Street. Fremont Street was an all-night, every-night party for tourists visiting Las Vegas. Freddy capitalized on the craziness that took place by selling frozen daiquiris and other spirits to the many people who flooded the area.

"Where are you going? What happened to you last night? How did you get hurt? Chance, what's going on? Is it about that woman who you saw at the restaurant?" Morgan asked nervously. Chance hadn't been back long before she heard him getting ready to leave once again.

"I gotta go meet Freddy. I'll be back as soon as I can," Chance said as he removed the pistol from the drawer next to his bed. He slid the cold steel into his waistline at his back.

"What are you meeting him about?"

"It's nothing. I just want to find out if Freddy's got some more work for me," Chance answered. He lied. After all he never told Morgan about the car that had tailed them after they left the restaurant in Henderson. He also never told her about the side work he was doing in tracking down the men who had

75

hurt her. Now, Chance was worried that someone was out to get him concerning his dealings with the Russians, which put Morgan in danger.

The party on Fremont Street was in full swing by the time Chance arrived. A live band played on a nearby stage, tourists drunkenly danced, and daredevils sped by on the zipline suspended right over the street, high above the party raging below them. He stood there for a moment listening to a rock 'n' roll song from the 80s. When the song ended, Chance turned and walked into Freddy's Bar. Once inside, he made his way to the bar and took a seat.

"What'll it be?" the bartender asked.

"Just a cola, and tell Freddy his nine o'clock is here," Chance said.

"Okay," the bartender replied. He placed a glass with ice in front of Chance and filled it with soda before walking away to deliver the message.

Chance looked around the bar at all the customers. At the back, he saw a familiar face. *What's he doing in town?* Chance asked himself. He then stood, grabbed his drink, and walked over toward the familiar man. The man wore black jeans, a black T-shirt, and black tactical boots. He was Bobby Smith, a former Navy SEAL whom Chance had the opportunity to work with on more than one occasion in Afghanistan.

"Bobby!" Chance spoke as he approached the man.

Bobby turned toward Chance when he heard his name, and he had a look of surprise on his face when he recognized the fellow operator. "Chance Hardway! I heard you were living somewhere around Las Vegas. How the hell are you?" Bobby asked as he stood to greet his old friend.

"I've been good, and you?"

"The same," Bobby answered.

"Are you here working?" Chance asked suspiciously.

"No, just partying for a few days. What about you?" Bobby asked, redirecting the conversation away from himself.

"Not right now, but I'm staying busy."

"That's good, man."

"Is he one of the other guys?" a man asked after walking up behind Bobby, who turned around to address the man.

"No. Uh, Daniel, this is Chance Hardway, an old Green Beret I worked with in Afghanistan. He lives here in Las Vegas now," Bobby explained.

The man caught on to what Bobby was hinting at, not to mention that he referred to him as Daniel and not West, his real name. "Oh, nice to meet you, Chance," West greeted as he reached out and shook Chance's hand.

"You too. Are you guys staying around here?" Chance asked. He knew the two men were expert operators. If one of them were here in Las Vegas, it wasn't really suspicious, but two of them together wasn't a coincidence. Freddy's Bar was the perfect place for people wanting to stay out of sight would go to get a drink.

"No, actually, I just got a text from Bill, another friend who's here, and he's on the Strip. We're heading over there to meet with him," Bobby said.

"Oh, that's too bad." Chance knew he was being lied to by his old friend. He also knew they were up to something, and there was at least one more operator somewhere.

"Maybe I'll see you later," Bobby offered as he walked out of the bar behind the other man.

"Maybe," Chance called back and then watched as the two men disappeared into the party crowd on Fremont.

"Freddy's ready for you," the bartender said when he returned.

"Thanks."

Leontii stood in his familiar spot in front of the window in his office, looking out over the city. He thought about the hit that was a few hours away from taking place. The hit would make national news. He had already called the Gorky family, who gave him, their trusted brigadier, the order to make it happen. The information the Romano family had outweighed any repercussions that may arise from the hit.

His cell phone vibrated in his pocket. He pulled it out and answered it. It was the call he had been waiting for.

"It's all set," Leontii said.

"Are you sure?" Edward Romano asked.

"Yes, you should have your boy back soon."

"That's good, and when I do, you'll get the information you need."

"I know, good night," Leontii replied, ending the call quickly.

Edward Romano put the cell phone on his desk and thought about everything for a moment. He looked over at Rico, one of his top men sitting in the chair next to him, waiting for orders.

"Has Hardway tried to leave Las Vegas?" Mr. Romano asked.

"Not that we know of. Our guys lost him after our contact in Las Vegas located him," Rico explained.

"I want him found. Tell our people not to lose him again!"

Freddy's office was small, to say the least. The large man sat behind a tiny desk in a small leather chair that had a view of the bar through a two-way mirror. Chance sat across from him in another equally small wooden chair.

"What's going on, Freddy? Things don't feel right," Chance confessed.

"What do you mean?" Freddy asked.

"I saw two operators in your bar just now. The kind that are real heavy hitters." Chance explained.

"That's a first for me but I didn't see them." Freddy stated.

"Okay, never mind that. Look, every time I show up to rough one of these Russians up, someone either shows up and kills them or beats me there and kills them. They had their chance to kill me on the boat but let me go instead. Now, I'm being followed, and I just bumped into some serious hired guns in your bar. I know you know something, and I want to know what it is," Chance expressed in a serious tone.

"Something big is about to happen," Freddy finally admitted.

"How do you know?"

"Cops can't keep their mouths shut. They're talking to informants, hookers, and anyone else who will listen. You know how some of them are, especially if they're trying to get laid."

"What are they saying?"

"Someone big is coming to Vegas, and a lot of people are getting ready for his arrival," Freddy answered.

"Who?"

Freddy leaned on the desk and looked directly at Chance. "If anyone in Las Vegas knew who it was, besides me that is, I would think it would be you. After all, you're the one who turned him over to the feds."

"Junior?"

"Jackpot!"

Lightning flashed, and thunder roared outside as dark clouds unleashed a heavy rain that covered the cabin. Henry looked out the bedroom window into the darkness outside and thought the water running down the glass made it appear as though the entire cabin was underwater. The bright flashes of light took him into a trance-like state, where he thought about his decision to testify against Junior in exchange for a new life. For a moment, he questioned whether it was the right thing to do, but then he looked down at the beautiful woman lying next to him. Jessica had come into his world and had somehow given him a new lease on life. If any good was going to come out of all of this, it would be Jessica.

"You should be asleep," she whispered as she rolled over and laid her head on his chest.

"I know, but I like looking at you more."

"Well, you should be thinking about how we have to get up in a few hours to fly out of here so that we can make it to Las Vegas on time."

"Marry me," Henry whispered, then pulled her close and kissed her softly. Jessica didn't know what to say back. She smiled, laid her head back down on his chest, and closed her eyes.

Bobby and West left the Strip and drove back to Frank's office early to go over the next day's operation. Both men also wanted to meet the rest of the team and get some sleep before the big day. When the men arrived, they found Frank, Ricky, and two other men standing in Frank's office around a table.

"I'm glad you two are back," Frank said as he directed the men to the table where a large map of Las Vegas was spread out over it.

"This is Avery and Brian," Ricky said, introducing the two new men to Bobby and West.

"I'm Bobby, and this is West. SEALs," Bobby said, introducing himself and his SEAL brother to the other two men.

"Raiders," Avery replied as all four men shook hands.

"Great, now that we're all one big happy family, how

about we discuss what we're doing tomorrow," Ricky stated and moved closer to the map.

Frank laid a photo of the target down on top of the map for everyone to see. "All right then. Here's the guy we're after."

When Chance left Freddy's, he slowly made his way through the party crowd to his truck. He sat there for a few minutes, working things out in his head. He still didn't know who was following him or why they were following him. He also didn't know why someone put him in a boat and sent it safely to shore right before blowing up Vasily Zlobin and his luxury yacht.

"Is Junior a part of everything that's going on? Are the Russians and Junior somehow connected to me? Why try to free Junior? Damn it! I can't figure this out!" Chance said in frustration as he started his truck.

He then thought about calling someone else, someone who could give him more information now that Chance had some information of his own to share.

The delivery driver, Trevor, dropped the pizzas off and left without much of a tip from the federal marshals. He wasn't too upset since he was already given three hundred dollars by the attractive woman in the parking lot. All Trevor had to do was say, "The pizza isn't gluten-free," loud enough for everyone inside the hotel room to hear him. When Trevor handed the pizzas to one of the men inside the room, he did what he was paid to do. As he pulled back out onto the highway, he said it once more out loud. "The pizza isn't gluten-free." He laughed loudly as he looked at the three crisp hundred-dollar bills in the passenger seat.

Junior ate his slice of pizza, thinking about what he heard the pizza delivery driver say. *Gluten-free,* he thought to himself.

It was a message from the family that they knew where he was, and he would soon be free.

Chance parked outside the convenience store and waited. After leaving Fremont Street, he had made a call to someone he felt he could trust, and after a few minutes of pleading with the one-time friend, the man relented and agreed to meet with Chance.

"You know I could get in a lot of trouble for just being seen with you," Parker Denton complained as he opened Chance's passenger door and sat down. Parker was a large, intimidating-looking man who had been with Metro for over twenty years. He had worked in almost every aspect of law enforcement, from patrol to vice and narcotics. He had also been Chance's training officer when Chance was hired. Now, Parker was a sergeant and Metro's liaison to the feds.

"I imagine you could," Chance agreed.

Parker stared out the window. "Why did you want to meet?"

"I got some information to share, but I need some from you first."

Parker shook his head. "That's not how it works. I'll give you what I can if your information is worth my time," he stated and drank from the water bottle he had brought with him.

Chance closed his eyes and took a second before speaking. "Fine. You guys got Junior coming into town in the morning," he said and waited for Parker to say something.

"Look, Chance, I'm not confirming or denying anything you tell me, so is that all you got to say?" Parker asked as he reached for the door handle.

"No, there are at least three hired guns in town, and the word on the street is that they're coming for Romano when you guys move him tomorrow," Chance said.

Parker removed his hand from the door and looked at Chance. "Go on."

"Well, if there's three that I know of, then there's probably three or even four more. The two I saw are heavy hitters. Just the two of them could take on ten, maybe twelve guys alone. Suppose there's six or more of them, and they're ready for your guys. In that case, it could be catastrophic for anyone around Junior tomorrow."

"How do you know it's Junior they've come into town to get?" Parker asked.

"I grabbed him and turned him over to the feds the other day in Philly."

"Okay, thanks for the information," Parker said and started to get out.

Chance gave Parker a disapproving glare. "Really, you got nothing for me?" He asked in a frustrated tone.

Parker paused and looked at his old friend. "Two dead and naked Russians were found in the desert. One Russian accountant was found dead in Philly. One Russian was killed in a hit at his house. Another is suspected of having been killed in an explosion on his boat. All these dead men have a few things in common. They were all Russian, they were all members of the Gorky crime family, and it's rumored that they all had some contact with a beautiful high-priced hooker named Morgan," Parker explained and stepped out of the truck.

"Anything else?" Chance asked.

"Yeah, and now I know they have one more thing in common."

"What's that?" Chance asked, already knowing the answer.

"They all have one man capable of killing them without leaving any trace of evidence. That one man just admitted, to a cop I might add, that he was in Philly, and that cop knows this man has a relationship with Morgan. He also knows Morgan was assaulted by a group of Russian men, and some of those

Russians are now dead. Catch you later, Chance Hardway," Parker said before getting out and slamming the door shut. Parker had enough to bring Chance in for questioning, but he felt that Chance was more valuable to him on the street. The man needed someone on the street passing him bits of information. Besides, deep down Parker still liked the guy.

CHAPTER 8
WEDDING BELLS

The jet soared high over the Nevada mountains on its way to Sin City. Marshal Jessica Wheeler looked at the sleeping Henry and thought about her life: the past, the present, and the future. She knew where she had been but didn't know where she was going. Life outside of the marshals' service was an unknown. Still, she was excited about it, especially if Henry was with her. When Henry started to wake, she turned her attention back to the sheet of paper on her lap.

Henry rubbed his eyes. "What are you doing?" He asked.

Jessica kept her head down. "Reading."

"Is it some important stuff?"

"Yes, I think your new name should be Wyatt William Preston," Jessica declared.

Henry chuckled. "Really, why?"

"I like the way it sounds. Besides, I like how Jessica Preston sounds."

Henry's jaw dropped. "Jessica Preston, wait, you mean that—"

Jessica put her finger to her lips to quiet her fiancé before one of the other agents on the plane heard what they were talking about. Henry sat up and glanced around the plane, then looked back at the beautiful woman sitting across from him.

"I love you," Henry whispered.

"I love you too," Jessica whispered back.

"We're on approach to McCarran. Make sure your seatbelts are fastened," Marshal Wilson advised. He sat next to Henry and fastened his seatbelt.

"What's the plan?" Henry asked.

"After we land, we'll drive to the federal courthouse and prance Henry around in front of the defense. After a few hours, we'll get back on the plane and fly back to the cabin. We should be home in time to order dinner," Wilson said.

"So Junior will be there," Henry said more than asked.

"Yes, but you don't need to worry about him. We'll have marshals everywhere."

"I'm not worried. I just want to see his face when I walk in. People like him believe they're untouchable, and they're not," Henry confidently proclaimed.

"Trust me. Junior doesn't think he has anything to worry about. He thinks the gun charge will just go away. The man he shot has already refused to testify, so Junior thinks he'll walk on the whole case," Jessica explained.

"But, with me witnessing him shoot the victim, you guys are charging him with the possession of a weapon charge or something like that," Henry replied, wanting to clarify his part. He had said he wasn't worried, but deep down, he was.

"Yes, Junior was charged with a burglary five years ago and a felony assault two years ago. Henry, you saw him in possession of a weapon that he fired at a known member of an organized crime organization. Junior himself is a known member of another criminal organization. We are charging him with possession of a weapon by a previous offender, and we'll try to add multi-state racketeering charges on top of it," Jessica further explained.

"Then, when this is over, I expect an invitation to the wedding," Dillon stated and then paused to look at the shock on the couple's faces. C'mon, I've known about the two of you for a while now. You two looked happy, so I just kept it to myself," Marshal Dillon Wilson confessed smugly.

"Thank you," Jessica said and then looked back at Henry, who was smiling as much as she was.

"Wyatt, just call me Wyatt," Henry announced proudly.

"That's as bad as Dillon," Wilson commented and laughed out loud along with the other two.

Junior woke when the rays of the sun broke through the crack in the dingy curtains. He knew the window overlooked the parking lot, but he had not been allowed outside the cheap motel room since he arrived. He grew tired of the faded green walls and the brown seventies furniture that adorned the room. He wasn't accustomed to such dismal accommodations. As he lay there staring at the chipped paint, he thought of being at the Emerald where he enjoyed the large suites, room service, and all the other amenities afforded to men of his status.

"Junior, it's time to get up! We're going to get you showered, fed, and into a car as quickly as possible," Marshal Westland ordered after walking into the room and uncuffing Junior's ankles.

"Man, I was dreaming I was in a much nicer place with three chicks catering to my every whim, if you know what I mean," Junior chuckled as he sat up and waited for his ankles to be freed.

Marshal Coleman and another marshal walked into the room. "I do, and that's something that will never happen for you after you're convicted. You're going away for a long time. Now, don't take too long in the shower either."

"Marshal Coleman, why you so mean?" Junior asked.

"Because you're a criminal who hurts innocent people. What makes it funny is that you're really nothing. If it weren't for who your father is, you'd be shoveling shit somewhere," Coleman answered as he threw a towel onto Junior's head.

"Asshole!" Junior yelled as he yanked the towel off.

Marshal Coleman laughed as he headed for the bathroom to make sure it was ready for the prisoner. Junior glared at the man as he moved toward the bathroom.

He'll see soon enough that I'm somebody, Junior thought to himself as he stood and began to undress.

Morgan made breakfast, brought the tray into the bedroom, and set it on the nightstand, but she did not awaken Chance right away. She found herself standing next to the bed staring at the man she was in love with as he lay there peacefully sleeping. Morgan knew he had been up to something over the past few weeks. She was sure that something had to do with her. When he returned to the RV last night, he was not himself, and she regretted not asking him what was on his mind.

"Sleepyhead, it's time to wake up," Morgan announced and slid herself onto the bed next to him.

"Good morning." Chance said back as he lifted his arm, inviting Morgan to lie close to him.

She made herself comfortable up alongside him. "Did you sleep well?"

"Yes, did you?"

"I did. Do you have plans for the day?" She asked.

"Yeah, I gotta check in on an old friend," he answered. Chance had plans to be near the federal courthouse when Junior arrived. He didn't know the route the marshals were taking, but he figured Junior would be one of the first prisoners to be arraigned this morning due to his popularity. Chance was going to be there when he arrived.

"Can we go to dinner later?" Morgan asked. She needed to talk to him and find out what he'd been up to lately.

"Sure," Chance answered and pulled her closer to him

Frank and the others worked out every detail of the plan before leaving for the ambush site. Each man had their orders and equipment and was ready to go. Frank and Ricky were the last two to walk out, and as Frank placed his bag into the front seat of the stolen sedan, Ricky walked toward him.

"The plan is a good one, as long as everyone sticks to it anyway," Ricky said with concern.

"I know, and they will," Frank said and shut the passenger door.

"I'm not talking about them." Ricky moved in front of his partner. He looked Frank in the eye and waited for him to say something.

"I'll do my part!"

"Are you sure? Your part of the plan is the most critical. If you fail, then everything we do out there today will be for nothing," Ricky reminded Frank with a tight tone in his voice.

"I'll do what I need to do. You just worry about yourself," Frank replied flatly. He brushed by Ricky, walked behind his car, got inside it, and sped away.

Leontii sat at his desk, eating breakfast, while Igor flipped through the television channels. The bodyguard was bored and wasn't accustomed to being up this early in the morning.

"I can't think this morning. Can you just choose a channel and leave it there, comrade?" Leontii asked.

"Yes, boss. I'm sorry. I'm not used to being awake this early," Igor explained.

"I know, and neither am I, but we must on this day."

"What are we to do?" Igor asked.

"We're going to be on the casino floor where the cameras can see us all morning. I don't want anyone assuming we had anything to do with what's going to happen in a few hours."

"So we're just to stand around all morning?" Igor asked.

"No, we'll make our rounds on the floor, stopping at the different gaming areas, completing our monthly walkthrough. Then, we'll meet with Boris at the White Sands Restaurant next to the high roller tables for lunch," the Brigadier explained and drank the last bit of tea from his cup.

"Boris is here?" Igor asked.

"He will be. He's keeping his travel plans secret until we know who's killing our people."

"Who do you think is killing our people?" Igor asked. It was a question that had been on his mind but one he'd never asked.

"Maybe the Romanians."

"They are here? I thought they were in California." Igor stood and walked to his boss's desk.

Leontii stood and put his suit coat on. "Maybe, we hear they are expanding. They may be attempting a hostile takeover."

"We are going to hit back, right?" Igor asked. The bodyguard knew that failure to retaliate was a sign of weakness in their type of business.

"We'll do whatever is needed to stop any takeover," Leontii assured his man and then walked out of the office.

The morning sun was already scorching the Nevada desert. Chance had found shade next to the building across from the courthouse, where he drank a cold cup of iced coffee that he had bought from the coffee shop on the corner. Chance knew something was going down, and he couldn't handle not knowing. Besides, he knew Junior was involved with the

Romano crime family and in one way or another with the Russian Mafia as well. No one outside of law enforcement knew that Junior was being brought in today. There wouldn't be any reporters, bystanders, or anyone else in the courtroom. Unfortunately, there were plenty of civilians on the street who were just getting started with their day, which could be a problem if something were going to happen.

The motorcade of three vehicles and ten marshals made their way on Interstate 515 toward E. Charleston Blvd. The route the marshals had planned called for them to exit onto E. Charleston Blvd. and take it to 15th St., where they planned to turn left on Bridger Ave. They would stay on Bridger until they got to 6th St., where they would pull up to the front of the Lloyd D. George US Courthouse and park in front of it. From there, they would escort Edward Romano Jr. into the courtroom.

Junior sat quietly, looking out the SUV's rear window at the desert landscape that rolled by quickly. He always liked the desert and preferred it over the busy streets of Philly, but Philly was where his family's business was located, so that was where he was required to be.

"It won't be long now, Junior," Marshal Westland announced from the front seat. Marshal Westland and the others wore tactical body armor, helmets, and earpieces, which was standard for any ground transport by the US Marshals who were transporting a high profile fugitive like Junior Romano. They carried an arsenal on them that would rival any soldier who was about to go into combat. Junior tried to make out what the marshals were saying but couldn't hear them very well, as they spoke quietly into their mics. It didn't matter that he couldn't listen to what was being said. He figured that at any minute, he would have a front-row seat where he could see everything.

The other motorcade of marshals was already on Interstate 15 and close to the exit for E. Charleston Blvd. Henry leaned toward Jessica, indicating he wanted to say something to her. Jessica was covered from head to toe in black tactical body armor. She held her AR-15 close to her chest at the ready as she leaned toward Henry.

"What?" she asked.

"Is it weird that I find you incredibly sexy in that outfit?" Henry asked and then sat up with a smile on his face.

Jessica smiled back and pressed her mic to give commands over her radio. Henry couldn't wait to start his new life with the woman sitting next to him. As the motorcade turned left onto Las Vegas Blvd., Henry adjusted his bulletproof vest and looked out the window at the buildings next to the street.

"We're turning right onto Gass Avenue and heading toward Sixth Street now," Jessica spoke into the mic attached to her chest. She was concerned about their plan for the day, but she didn't let Henry know it. Instead, she appeared confident and ready.

Chance stood there leaning against the corner of the building, watching courthouse employees going in and out. He was enjoying the last little bit of his iced coffee when his cell phone vibrated in his front pocket. He threw the empty cup into the trash, reached into his pocket, and pulled it out. He looked at the caller ID and smiled when he saw who it was.

"Hello," Chance greeted.

"What are you doing here?" Parker asked.

The corners of Chance's mouth turned up. "I figured you'd be here," he replied.

"Answer my question, Hardway," Parker ordered.

"I'm just a concerned citizen who likes to keep up with the criminal justice system in Las Vegas. Besides, there's no law saying I can't be out here," Chance explained with a wide smile on his face.

"Are you armed?" Parker asked.

"No, I'm not." Chance took his cell phone from his ear, lifted his shirt, and turned around slowly, knowing that Parker and probably some marshals were watching from a distance.

"Stay out of the way," Parker said sternly into the phone and ended the call.

Chance placed his phone back into his pocket. He looked down Las Vegas Boulevard to his left and then to his right. It was on his right side where he saw something that caught his eye.

Ricky watched the plastic newspaper bin that he had placed on the corner of 6th Street and Bridger Ave. The container was red, white, and slightly abused. Ricky found it abandoned near the Las Vegas Strip and decided to use it. The explosive charge he had hidden inside was enough to take out the entire corner of the building it sat next to, as well as any vehicle that was passing by when he detonated it. He waited patiently with his hand on the remote trigger for the target vehicle to enter the kill zone.

Frank sat inside the stolen sedan he had parked along the street a few blocks down from 6th Street. He waited patiently for Ricky's signal. He adjusted his body armor, checked his weapon, and held the mask he was to use to cover his face during the ambush. The police lieutenant had paid a hundred thousand dollars to a contact he had in the marshals' service. The paid contact provided Frank with the route and the time they were to arrive in front of the courthouse. He looked down the street and saw West, Brian, and Avery parked on the other side of the intersection. Frank couldn't see Bobby, who positioned away from the ambush site. Still, he believed that

Bobby, like himself and the others, was waiting for Ricky's signal.

Chance walked toward the odd-looking newspaper box that seemed out of place near the courthouse. Usually, it wouldn't have caught his attention, but it was beaten, broken, and was one commonly found on the Strip, closer to the casinos where tourists opened them to retrieve sexually explicit advertisements. It wasn't something generally found on the street near the federal courthouse. As he got closer, he heard approaching cars. He paused and looked behind him. Coming up the street was a black SUV.

"Team one is pulling up in front of the courthouse now," Jessica advised over the radio.

"Roger, and Team two is turning on to 6th Street now," Marshal Westland said in turn.

Chance watched as three SUVs screeched to a stop once they pulled up in front of the courthouse. The doors flew open, and the marshals inside began to exit the vehicles. Down at the other end of the street, another set of SUVs turned onto 6th Street from Bridger Ave.

Ricky waited until the precise moment. When he saw the doors open of one of the SUVs parked in front of the courthouse, and the other set of SUVs passed in front of the bin, he detonated the bomb.

Chance saw the flash and was violently thrown up and backward into the air by the blast. He landed on his back, and for a moment, he was dazed. Chance couldn't hear anything, but as he lay there trying to collect himself, he kept his eyes open and saw black smoke rising from an SUV on its side a short distance from him. People ran about, trying to get to cover, while others injured by the bomb littered the sidewalk and the street.

CHAPTER 9
THE HIT

Ricky's explosion sent the lead SUV into the air and onto its side. The four marshals exiting it were dead before the large vehicle landed back on the ground. Marshal Westland and his driver were feeling the effects of the blast. Their vehicle was behind the first SUV, which took the direct hit. Junior found his way to the floorboard and remained there. He knew the attack was only beginning, and it was time for him to sit tight and wait it out.

Jessica and her team dropped down and took cover while directing their attention to the area around them. Henry stayed in the back seat of the SUV but kept his eyes on Jessica. He wasn't going to let her out of his sight.

While the smoke cleared, Ricky dropped behind his M 249 machine gun and aimed for the second SUV's hood, in Junior's convoy. He pulled the trigger, and the sound of automatic fire echoed off the surrounding buildings. Marshal Westland saw the rounds entering the engine compartment directly in front of him. The rounds Ricky fired into the SUV engine were risky to say the least, but he had to stop the SUV from advancing forward. Ricky had determined that the man behind the M 249 had to be an accurate shot, and he didn't trust anyone else but himself to do it. He then directed his fire to the SUV carrying the witness. He flattened the front tires and disabled the engine just as he had done to the other one.

"I need cover!" Westland shouted into his radio as he opened the passenger door and jumped out. He then opened the rear passenger door and pulled Junior outside. He dragged the young man toward the building to his right. The marshals from the third vehicle in Westland's team ran up to his vehicle and looked for the shooter through the dark smoke. Westland and Junior were nearly at one of the building doors when a bullet ricocheted off a building and found its way into Marshal Westland's shoulder.

"Damn it!" Westland yelled. He was hit with another round in his hip. The wounded marshal and Junior broke through a shop door and fell onto the tile entry inside.

Ricky saw the other marshals making their way toward the second vehicle and decided it was time to signal the others. Marshal Coleman had made his way up toward Westland's vehicle and took cover next to a concrete bench. Ricky grabbed the trigger for the second explosive and squeezed it quickly.

Coleman looked under the bench and saw the backpack and then a sudden flash of light. He never heard the explosion; the marshal and his team were dead in less than a second.

The second explosion blew out the windows in the buildings close to the blast, but more importantly, it was the signal that Frank and the others were waiting for. Frank covered his face, hit the gas, and sped toward the courthouse. West and the other men did the same.

Jessica and her team were still on a knee when she grabbed her radio. She looked around at the fires and smoke from the explosions down the street. Her vehicle was disabled, and she and the others needed to get off the street and into the courthouse.

"We move into the courthouse on my command!" she yelled into the mic.

"No!" Parker ordered over the radio.

"Why?" Jessica asked.

"Let us get our team in place to cover you before you come inside," Parker instructed.

"Then get there! We need to get off the street!"

Parker and his people were on the fourth floor of the courthouse when the first explosion detonated. He and the others were still making their way downstairs when the second one went off.

Ricky was still on the rooftop, firing the M249 at the marshals in both convoys. The suppressive fire killed one more marshal and wounded another. The last one who was still able to fight in Westland's motorcade had taken cover behind a concrete bench.

Jessica watched the courthouse's front for the others to come out and cover her and her team. It seemed like an eternity before she saw the doors open and two men run outside.

"Get ready!" Jessica said as she looked back toward Henry.

"I'm ready!"

"Now!" Parker yelled over the radio.

"I'll go first. You and Henry run for it when I give you the go-ahead." Dillon ordered.

"Okay, but be careful!" Jessica yelled over the sound of the automatic gunfire.

Marshal Dillon Wilson stood from the driver's side and ran out onto the sidewalk. He dropped to a knee and raised his AR-15 to cover Jessica and Henry while they ran for the door.

Dillon looked back and yelled, "Now!"

Jessica stood just in time to see a bullet enter her partner's head. She watched in awe as Marshal Dillon Wilson's lifeless body dropped to the concrete in front of her.

"Jessica!" Henry shouted as a masked gunman wearing body armor came toward her.

The shooter was Avery, and he was determined to be the one who was credited with killing the target.

It took her a moment to realize the man was firing his weapon at her. The gunman's bullets hit her bulletproof vest, surprising her and pushing her back against the opened door. She felt pain in her arm and looked down and saw blood. The marshal in the front passenger seat took a shot to the head and dropped his pistol into the back seat, right before he slid downward out of the vehicle.

Henry looked around and saw the marshal in the passenger seat was dead. He reached down and grabbed the dead man's gun, then quickly pointed it at the approaching shooter who had shot Jessica. Henry pulled the trigger and held it as the rounds continued to hit the advancing attacker.

Avery fell to the concrete, but he was not done. He raised his gun once more and aimed it at Henry. Henry tried to shoot again, but the pistol was empty.

Jessica may have been hit, but she wasn't out of the fight. She drew her pistol from her side holster and shot the man before he could kill Henry.

Parker and the others saw the attacking shooters and decided to move outside, where the fight was taking place. Parker was the first to open the door, and as he did so, he and the others were pelted with automatic gunfire. Bullets shattered the glass of the doors. Parker was hit twice, once in the arm and once in the calf. He dropped onto his stomach and fired back at the shooter, who stood on the sidewalk firing an automatic machine gun at the courthouse's entrance.

Brian smiled when he saw the men inside fall to the ground. He held the M249 solid against his shoulder and used a short burst of fire to control his aim. He looked back and signaled Frank and West to move toward the target. Frank didn't hesitate. He rushed the SUV while West covered him from behind.

After Chance had regained his senses, he took cover behind a car opposite the SUV that was now under attack. He looked around for a weapon to no avail as gunfire continued to echo up and down both ends of the street. Cops were being killed, and that wasn't something he would allow to happen, even if he didn't have a weapon. He moved from his position of cover toward one of the two men in the street. Chance ran up behind the unsuspecting gunmen and leaped into the air. He wrapped his arms around the man's neck, and as he and the man fell to the road, Chance used his weight and the pressure he was applying to break the man's neck. He then grabbed the pistol attached to the man's chest and ran for the SUV.

West didn't know what had happened. He felt no pain; he just lay there on the road, helplessly watching as bullets bounced off the pavement around him.

Henry desperately pulled at Jessica as he tried to get her back inside the SUV. She was bleeding badly. She needed to get to a hospital soon. Henry grabbed her around the bottom of her vest and pulled her up and into the SUV. Once he got her inside, he closed the door and laid her down flat on the back seat.

"Stay with me, baby!" Henry pleaded.

He reached for the other door to close it, but he wasn't quick enough. Frank had done his job as planned. He got to the target, raised his gun, and was about to pull the trigger when suddenly he felt rounds hitting him in the back. He spun around and fired his gun, but Chance was fast. He grabbed Frank's gun hand and redirected his aim.

Chance then placed the gun he had taken off the first man under the assassin's chin and pulled the trigger.

Lieutenant Frank Carter didn't know what had happened. He looked into Chance's eyes and slowly dropped to the ground where he died.

Chance ran in front of the SUV and made his way toward the gunmen who kept the others locked down inside the courthouse. Chance repeatedly fired at the shooter until the man dropped to the ground.

Junior found himself lying next to an unconscious Marshal Westland. He figured this was an opportunity he couldn't pass up. He reached into Westland's pockets, removed the handcuff keys, and freed himself. Junior then stood and saw the melee unfolding outside. He looked back at the wounded marshal and came up with a plan.

Chance ran toward the courthouse entrance, where he was met with marshals coming at him with their weapons pointed right at him. He was ordered to stop and to drop his gun.

"No, let him by!" Parker ordered.

"You okay?" Chance asked as he assisted Parker to the ground and knelt next to his wounded friend.

"You were right," Parker admitted as Chance applied pressure to his friend's leg.

"I won't say I told you so, but I did," Chance muttered.

"I know. Now, where's Junior?"

"I don't know," Chance answered. The sound of sirens grew louder as the emergency vehicles got closer to the scene.

Ricky was on the rooftop, surveying the area for more targets, when suddenly he saw a marshal making his way down the sidewalk. The M249 had a few more rounds left. After he carefully took aim, he fired another hail of bullets at the new target. He kept firing until the man dropped to the ground. Ricky then felt his cell phone vibrating in his pocket.

"Do we have everyone? Did we get the target?" Ricky asked after answering the call.

"No! Everything has gone to hell. You and I are the only ones left. I'm getting out of here!" Bobby explained excitedly as he raced away from the skirmish in the getaway car.

Ricky ended the call, rushed to the side of the building, and used the rope he had brought to rappel into the alley. When he got to the ground, he rushed to his car and casually drove away.

It was six in the evening when Chance was finally released from the hospital and the FBI's custody, who had taken over the investigation into the ambush. He had been treated for his injuries, which included a concussion that was either moderate or severe. The severity of the concussion depended on who you asked. This evening, it was both the patient and the doctor who had a difference of opinion regarding the severity of the brain injury. Chance also had some minor scrapes and bruises that he initially refused treatment for, but a very angry and upset Morgan arrived and insisted he get treated. Chance knew Morgan wasn't taking no for an answer, and by the look on Morgan's face when she arrived, he figured it was better to do as she insisted.

"How are you feeling?" Morgan asked as they entered the elevator.

"Pretty good," Chance answered and then leaned down and kissed her.

Morgan watched Chance push the button for the twelfth floor instead of the first floor. "Where are we going?"

"I gotta see Parker."

Edward Romano sat in his living room, waiting for any information about his son to come in. No one knew anything, and his calls to the department of justice went unanswered. He was growing impatient, and not knowing anything was getting the better of him. He wanted to talk to someone, but there was no one in the room but him. He just sat there, flipping the channels between the different national news stations covering the Las Vegas shooting.

Ricky drove all day and planned on going all night. The closer he got to Mexico, the better he felt. He had what was left of his money, and right now, that was all he needed. He watched every car that drove by or behind him. He kept his speed down and made sure he stayed in his lane. Right now, he couldn't and didn't want to draw unwanted attention.

Leontii, Boris, and Igor sat in the Emerald's office, waiting for Edward Romano Sr. to call with the name of the man they were looking for. The Russians didn't know whether the Philadelphia crime boss would call or not, but they hoped for the best.

"If his son is dead, he won't give us the name he has, and he will blame us for his son's death," Boris advised as he walked to the liquor cabinet to refill his glass. The Russian had arrived earlier in the day as planned and had had lunch with Leontii and Igor. They watched the news all afternoon, hoping to get something about who was killed. They also sent some of their own people to the scene to see if they could get any information.

"I know," Leontii replied as he held up his glass for Boris to refill it.

Parker was lying back in his bed, while the TV on the wall played out the day's events, when Chance walked in. Morgan stayed outside in the hallway. The veteran cop looked up and shook his head at the sight of the man darkening his doorway. Chance stood there but didn't say anything; he just smiled.

"I know. You told me so," Parker mumbled.

"I wasn't going to say that," Chance replied as he moved closer to the bed.

"You saved a lot of lives today, including mine." Parker reached out and shook Chance's hand.

Chance returned the gesture. "You're welcome."

Parker shook his head. "I didn't say thank you."

"I know, but still, you're welcome."

The two of them laughed.

"You okay?" Chance asked.

"I will be. They are doing some minor surgery on me in the morning. I'm supposed to be sleeping right now. They gave me something for the pain and hoped it would put me to sleep, but it hasn't worked yet," Parker explained as he laid his head back onto his pillow.

"Do you know what happened today? Can you tell me anything?" Chance asked.

Parker slowly started to close his eyes. "I'll tell you because you saved my life, and I'm feeling pretty good right now."

Chance smirked. "I'll take whatever I can get."

"The man you killed next to the car was Lieutenant Frank Carter."

"What!" Chance exclaimed.

"Yeah, and Junior is dead too."

"Wait, what?"

"Yeah, I'm full of good news, aren't I? Apparently, Junior put on some marshal's gear and walked out into the open where he was shot and killed by one of the men who hit us. The witness, who you stopped Frank from killing, was the target."

"So, Junior wasn't the target but ended up being the one who got killed," Chance said, clarifying what he was just told by a drugged-up and groggy Parker.

"Yes," Parker acknowledged.

"What do you think will happen now?" Chance asked.

Parker lazily shrugged. "I think the Russians and the Romano family will be looking for you now."

"That's crazy," Chance suggested in return.

In the hallway, Morgan moved closer to the door when she heard Parker mention the Russians.

"Crazy? What's crazy is going after the Russians who raped

and beat your girlfriend." Parker slurred as he began to slide between being awake and sleeping.

Chance placed his hand on Parker's forearm. "You're not thinking right. I'll come back later," he said. Chance started to leave but heard Parker once more. He stopped and looked at his old friend.

"Why did you take the evidence from the locker?" Parker asked right before he passed out.

Chance thought about what Parker had said and once again he was reminded of why he had left Metro. Unfortunately, that was a conversation that would have to wait. Chance turned back toward the door and found Morgan standing there.

"What was he talking about with the Russians?"

Edward Romano listened intently. The reporter told her viewers that Junior was among the dead in today's early morning shootout that took place in front of the Lloyd D. George Federal Courthouse. One tear slowly dripped down his cheek as he looked at a body bag with what he believed to be his son being lifted into a white-panel van. He closed his eyes and remembered his son for a moment. He then stood and threw his glass of whiskey at the TV screen, shattering them both. Two bodyguards promptly ran in from the hall.

"Boss, you okay in here?" one of the men asked.

"No! Arrange a meeting with the Russians in Las Vegas. I'm going there to get my son."

Leontii answered his phone after the third ring. He had just heard the news about Junior.

"Yes," Leontii said into the receiver and then listened to the man on the other end of the call. "Very well. I'll make the arrangements."

"Who was it?" Igor asked after his boss finished the call.

"The Romanos want a meeting here in Las Vegas."

Bobby sat in the hotel room alone and in the dark. He didn't know what to do or where to go. All he knew was that the feds were looking for accomplices from the shooting. He lay back on the bed and closed his eyes, pondering whether he could have done more to help the others during the shooting. He felt that if he had been there in the fight, he could have done more than waiting down the street in the getaway car.

"No one saw me. I'm sure of that, but I don't know for sure. I gotta get some sleep. In the morning, I'll have more clarity," Bobby told himself as he started to drift off to sleep. Suddenly, he sat up.

"What about Chance Hardway? He saw me with West. I guess I'm going back to Las Vegas to tie up a loose end, and Ricky is going with me, whether he likes it or not."

CHAPTER 10
WANTED

Chance and Morgan made it back to his place by nine o'clock. The ride home from the hospital had been quiet. Chance never spoke about the Russians after they left the hospital. When they entered the RV, he immediately walked into the bathroom and showered. Morgan decided right then and there that the two of them would have a conversation no matter what. Chance was keeping something to himself, and it was time for her to know what it was, especially since it involved her. Morgan grabbed a beer from the refrigerator, poured herself a glass of wine, took a seat on the leather sofa, and waited.

Leontii and Boris sat in the office, waiting patiently for Igor to get off the phone. After the phone call from Edward Romano Sr., the Russians had contacted the Underground. They offered a reward for information about the shooting. The reward started low, but Leontii doubled it every thirty minutes until someone finally called.

"You won't believe this," Igor stated after he ended the call.

"What won't I believe?" Leontii asked.

"Junior was killed by the men we hired to kill the witness.

He put on a marshal's vest and walked out into the open and was shot," Igor explained.

"Great!" Leontii yelled and then stood and walked to the window.

"There's more," Igor stated.

"What is it?" Boris answered when Leontii did not.

"Hardway killed Carter when he was about to shoot the witness."

"Anything else?" Boris asked.

"Not yet."

Ricky turned the car around right before getting to the US and Mexico border. The call from Bobby concerned him. Although Ricky hadn't been seen at the shooting or by anyone alive in Las Vegas, Bobby had been seen by Chance Hardway. If Hardway said something to the police about Bobby, then Bobby, in turn, might say something about Ricky. Before he got off the phone with his accomplice, the two decided that they needed to make sure Hardway couldn't say anything to anyone.

Henry stayed at Jessica's bedside until she woke. The surgery to repair her wound was successful. The US Marshals Service requested that Henry leave and return to the cabin in Lake Tahoe immediately. He refused until he knew his fiancée was going to be okay. No one knew about their relationship except for the late Marshal Dillon Wilson. Henry had been able to keep it a secret. When the marshals service demanded he get back on the plane to leave Las Vegas, Henry insisted they complete a full bomb sweep on the aircraft and the car he was to ride in. He also faked being injured and was given a CT scan of his head, shoulder, and torso to help prolong his time at the hospital until he knew Jessica was out of surgery.

"What are you still doing here?" Jessica managed to ask. She had been sedated and was drifting between consciousness and unconsciousness.

"I wanted to make sure you were going to be all right before I left," Henry whispered. He then looked back at the recovery room door before leaning over and kissing her lightly.

"I love you," she whispered before drifting off to sleep.

"I love you too."

"I'm okay," Marshal Martin Westland assured as he ran his hand over the back of Jenny's head.

Jenny had called her brother, Tom, after hearing her husband had been shot. She asked Tom, who was a pilot, to get her to Las Vegas on his plane faster than a commercial flight, which he could, and he did. Jenny couldn't stop crying ever since she saw the countless amateur videos of the shootout on TV.

"Marty, I thought I was going to lose you," she admitted through sobs.

"I know, but I'll never let that happen. I'm never leaving you again."

"You mean..."

"Yes," he said. "I think it's time to leave this job to the younger generation."

"Thank goodness!"

Chance walked out of the shower and found Morgan waiting for him. He knew he couldn't avoid the topic of the Russians anymore. It was time to come clean about what he had been up to over the past few weeks.

"What time is it?" Chance asked as he sat next to Morgan, who undoubtedly was on her second, maybe a third glass of wine.

"Maybe it's time for you to talk to me," Morgan stated as she took another sip of her Merlot.

"It is. Well, after what happened to you, I decided to go after the men who did it," Chance confessed. He looked at her and waited for her to say something.

"Did you kill them?" Morgan asked as she used her hand to swirl the wine in her glass without looking up at him.

"No. Well, I did kill Victor, but I didn't plan on it… or maybe I did. I really don't know, but I wasn't bothered by it. As for the others, I just wanted to hurt them, like they hurt you." Chance grabbed the bottle of beer off the table and took a long drink.

"Tell me everything. I want to know what you did to them. Everything, don't leave anything out."

Freddy sat at his dining room table, watching the Underground message board. Someone somewhere was offering a lot of money for any information that wasn't being released to the public regarding the early morning shooting. He didn't know who it was, not yet anyway.

"Do you need anything, Sugar?" Candi asked after she walked into the room and placed her arms around the large man's shoulders. Candi was Freddy's girl. She was tiny, beautiful, and catered to his every need.

"No, I'm good for now," Freddy answered as he reached around and pulled her in front of him, where he eased her onto his lap.

"What are you looking at?" Candi asked. She made herself more comfortable on Freddy's large leg while pretending to be interested in what he was doing.

Freddy enjoyed Candi's company. He also never had to worry about her seeing anything because she wouldn't understand what she was looking at. Freddy liked Candi solely for her body and the attention she gave him and not her brains, which he believed she had very little of. Freddy always had to help Candi update her phone software, log into her different online accounts, and download the newest apps on her phone.

"Nothing," Freddy answered as he rubbed her back. He smiled in amusement as he watched her stare at the screen intently.

"What does that mean?" Candi pointed at a green box on the right side of the screen. Freddy leaned closer and saw that someone else had some information.

Morgan listened to Chance tell how he had been administering some street justice to the men who had raped, beat, and cut her. When he was finished, she looked him in the eye, caressed his neck, and kissed his cheeks. She realized he had been carrying a heavy burden. For the past three years, Morgan had felt the situation she was in was her problem, not anyone else's, and most certainly not Chance's. It was a problem that was created when she got involved with the Russians, but now it was time to tell him everything.

The Russian boss sat there with Boris on one side of the table and Igor on the other. The three of them were trying to figure a way out of their situation.

"The Romano family will come and demand reparations for Junior's death," Leontii stated and then looked back and forth between the other two men. "The men we hired killed the wrong man. How can we fix this?"

"Give them someone else to blame," Boris suggested.

Igor turned his head and shrugged his shoulders, then asked, "Who?"

"Hardway. He's the one who interfered with the hit," Boris answered.

"I will kill Hardway!" Igor replied. The Russian was eager to kill the man responsible for his brother's death.

"No, the Romanos will want him. They'll deal with him in the way they think is right," Boris explained. He stood and walked around the room, thinking. "How do we get to Hardway?"

"The girl," Leontii answered and walked to the safe. He then knelt, spun the dial for the combination, opened it up, and took something out.

"How do we get to the girl? No one has seen her," Igor stated.

Leontii held up a thumb drive. "With this."

Freddy clicked the green icon in the corner of the screen and saw the new advertisement.

"Selling information on the murder of Juan Muñoz."

"Wow!" Freddy said after he read the words.

"What is it?" Candi asked.

"Someone is trying to collect on something big," Freddy explained.

"How big?"

"Million or two," Freddy answered.

"That is big. Who's Juan Muñoz?"

"Well, he was the son and the right hand of Hector Muñoz."

"The drug cartel czar from Colombia?" Candi asked excitedly.

"Yeah, Juan Muñoz was found murdered in a rundown hotel room near Henderson a few years ago."

"Was he killed by another cartel?"

"That's just it, no one knows, Candi. His murder is still unsolved," Freddy said just as someone answered the ad.

The reply read: "2.5"

"Wow! It looks like someone is offering to buy the information," Freddy stated and stood with a surprised look on his face.

"Now what?" Candi asked.

"Well, if the seller agrees to the offer, he or she will respond with a yes or a no. Then the money gets deposited by the buyer into an account I have set up overseas. When they both text the Underground that both sides are satisfied with the information and there are no disputes, the money is released to the seller—minus my commission of ten percent."

"Who do you think is selling the information?"

"I don't know, but I'm pretty sure that Hector Muñoz is the buyer."

"Who do you think killed Juan Muñoz?" Candi asked.

After Morgan was finished telling him what had happened, Chance sat there looking at her as tears streamed down her face. He now knew why Morgan could never stop working for the Russians.

"I'm so sorry I never said anything before." Morgan dropped her head to her chest. "I never meant to be whore!" she exclaimed and cried uncontrollably.

"You're not!" Chance declared. He grabbed her and pulled her against him. He then picked her up and carried her to bed. The two of them fell asleep in the other's arms.

When Morgan awoke in the morning, she walked into the living room and found Chance there looking at his cell phone.

"Would you like to go out for breakfast?" Morgan asked as she moved closer to him.

Chance looked up and answered, "No, we have something more pressing to take care of this morning." He then looked back down at his phone and read the text messages from the Underground.

"What's wrong?" Morgan asked after seeing the concerned look on Chance's face.

"I think someone is coming for you."

PART II

CHAPTER 11
A TRIP DOWN MEMORY

Three Years Ago

The taxi dropped her off earlier than expected and quickly drove away after she paid her fare. Now, Morgan stood in the Stay and Play Motel parking lot looking for the client's room number. The rundown motel was on the outskirts of Henderson, Nevada, and it appeared as though no one was renting any of the rooms. There were no cars in the parking lot. Only one room had lights on inside, yet the sign on the side of the building indicated no vacancies. It was already late in the evening, and Morgan was in a hurry to get the call over with. She wanted to get back to her apartment, pack her belongings, and leave Las Vegas once and for all. This evening, the client was a referral from Joshua Campbell, the owner of the Emerald Hotel and Casino. Morgan had first refused the call, but Campbell was insistent and offered her five times her going rate for two hours of her time. Ten thousand dollars was more than enough money to get her out of town and get her set up somewhere until she found legitimate work.

"You can do this! This is the last time," Morgan whispered

and walked toward the one room with the light on. She stood in front of the door, took a deep breath, and knocked.

Juan Muñoz was excited to meet the girl Joshua Campbell had arranged for him. Juan had spent a lot of money on this one, so he was eager to meet her. He had trouble concentrating on the drug deal he had completed earlier in the day. It had been very profitable for the Muñoz Cartel, and Juan's father was pleased when he spoke to him on the phone afterward. He was still thinking about how happy his father was with him when he heard her knock on the door. Juan rushed over and opened it.

Morgan greeted him with a smile. "Hi! I'm Morgan."

"Hello. Yes, I'm Juan," Juan replied as he eagerly looked her over. He was pleased, to say the least. She was beautiful, and she wore a tight red cocktail dress that accentuated her curvy figure. Morgan took the time to look her new client over as well. He was tall, thin, and dressed very well. His eyes were dark brown, and his skin was golden brown.

"Are you going to invite me in?" Morgan asked after a few awkward seconds.

"Yes! Please come in," Juan said and then stepped to the side and opened the door further.

Morgan slowly and cautiously walked into the small room. She quickly surveyed her surroundings and took note of a black bag sitting on the dresser. Next to the bag was an elegantly wrapped red-and-white gift box.

"Are you in town for business or pleasure?" Morgan laughed. It was a common phrase that she, along with everyone else, used to break the ice with someone new.

"Both, actually."

"Is your business in Henderson or Las Vegas?"

"You ask a lot of questions," Juan stated and then locked the door.

Morgan gave a half smile. "I'm sorry. I don't mean to pry. I was just—"

"It's okay. I'm just nervous. It's my first time," Juan said, but it was a lie. He was not nervous, and it most certainly was not his first time with a prostitute.

Morgan walked over and kissed his cheek while softly rubbing the back of his neck. "Don't be nervous. I'll be gentle,"

"I have something for you," Juan blurted and quickly pulled away. He walked to the dresser, picked up the gift box, and handed it to Morgan.

"What's in it?"

"That's a surprise."

Morgan smiled and opened the box while occasionally looking up at her client, who appeared to be excited as he watched her. Once the wrapping paper was removed, Morgan carefully pulled off the top of the brown box and took out the white tissue paper. Underneath the paper was a black lace teddy and black high heel shoes. She now knew why Campbell had asked what her shoe size was when she agreed to the date earlier in the day.

"I hope they fit. I spent a lot of time this afternoon looking for them," Juan confessed and then moved closer to her so he could help her take the shoes out of the box. He laid the box with the teddy on the dresser.

"They're very nice!" Morgan said excitedly, but it wasn't a sincere expression of excitement. Over the years, Morgan had gotten used to pretending to be enthusiastic when given a gift from a client, even when it wasn't something to get excited about, like a pair of twelve-hundred-dollar pumps that she was now holding in her hands. It was a gift from a man who had an apparent foot fetish. Morgan watched as Juan caressed the shoes while looking down at her feet.

Juan led her toward the bathroom. "Please go into the bathroom and change. I'll wait here on the bed."

"Okay, I'll be just a few minutes," Morgan said. She walked into the small, outdated bathroom, shut the door, and locked it. She looked in the mirror and pondered how she had ever gotten to this point in her life.

Once Morgan closed the door, Juan rushed to the dresser and opened his bag. He reached inside and took out his handcuffs, knife, and hacksaw, then gently pulled out his black leather mask. He pulled it over his head and took off his clothes. Juan had killed nine women already, and tonight, Morgan was going to be number ten. He relived each kill as he carefully but quickly placed the photos of the other victims around the bed. He had to get things into place before the girl came back out. Usually, the serial killer, who Juan was, had more time to prepare. Unfortunately, the store clerk had taken longer than expected to wrap the shoes, and then the girl showed up early, both of which put him behind schedule.

Before Morgan started to change her clothes, she used her phone and looked on the internet for foot fetishes, where she found pictures that made her sick. "Why?" she whispered and then started to remove her dress. Suddenly, she realized she had left the lace teddy in the box on the dresser.

Juan was standing next to the bed with the hacksaw in one hand and his handcuffs in the other when the bathroom door opened. Morgan stood there, not moving as she looked at the naked masked man standing in front of her.

She felt as though time had slowed. Morgan saw Juan, the handcuffs, the hacksaw, and the photos of the other women on the bed. Juan looked at her, and she looked back at him. Then, both looked at the knife on the dresser.

Juan dropped his handcuffs and went after her with the hacksaw. She quickly grabbed the knife and held it out in front of her. Juan swung his saw wildly, but in doing so, he tripped on the corner of the bed and fell forward onto Morgan. He gasped as he felt the blade enter deep into his right lung.

Morgan stepped back into the bathroom doorway as the masked man stood to his feet and slowly started for the room door. He took about three steps and reached for the doorknob but collapsed on the stained carpet before he could open it. The woman who was to be the victim was now the executioner, and she remained in the doorway, unable to move. She just stood there, looking down at the dead man.

Joshua Campbell got to the Stay and Play Motel at about one o'clock in the morning. He got there as quickly as possible after his man called and told him what had occurred between Juan Muñoz and the hooker. By the time he arrived, Morgan was gone, and Juan Muñoz was lying dead on the floor.

"Show me," Campbell ordered his man.

The man Campbell had hired to film Juan's encounter with Morgan picked up his camera and played the footage for the casino owner. The two of them watched the entire video from the time Morgan arrived until the time she ran out of the room, stepping over Juan Muñoz, the one and only heir to the Muñoz Cartel, as she did.

"Download it to this thumb drive," Campbell ordered and handed the cameraman a silver-colored memory stick. He then walked over and pulled Juan's mask off. He picked up the photos and hacksaw and put everything belonging to the killer back into the black bag. Campbell knew Juan Muñoz was the infamous Vegas Handicapper. The serial killer had been terrorizing Nevada and its neighboring states for the past two years.

The killer received the odd moniker after one of his victims' feet was found in a public garbage can at Lake Mead. A local writer created the strange nickname after writing an article about it titled: *The Latest* and *Newest, Las Vegas Handicapper*. The article insinuated that the victim could possibly be alive but without one of her feet. Unfortunately, the rest of the victim's body was found in the famous lake with both of her feet cut off, but not before the nickname took.

THE PRESENT

That night Campbell had deleted the original copy of the incident and sent the cameraman away, only to have him killed later. He also took and hid the black bag and its contents, an insurance policy for the future if he ever needed it. He then cleaned the room and the knife of fingerprints. He left Juan Muñoz lying on the floor. The murderer of Juan Muñoz had never been found. For three years, Campbell kept the thumb drive of Morgan killing Juan as leverage to keep her working for him. After Campbell was killed, it became the property of the new casino manager, Leontii Adamovich.

Leontii just sold it to Hector Muñoz, the Muñoz drug cartel leader and the father of Juan Muñoz.

"Mariana!" Hector yelled. The drug czar sat in a leather chair in his mansion in Colombia, replaying the video of his son's murder.

"Yes, Papá?" Mariana said as she walked up and stood behind her father to look at the video.

Hector pointed to the video. "Find this woman and prepare our plane. We're going to Las Vegas."

"Papá, we should stay focused on the business and not—"

"Now, Mariana! Do as I say. I'm the head of this family, not you! This woman will be killed!" Hector yelled.

CHAPTER 12
FIRE SALE, EVERYTHING MUST GO!

When Chance saw the Underground text message where someone offered to sell information about Juan Muñoz's killer, he immediately told Morgan to stay inside and out of sight until he got back. Morgan was scared, and her first instinct was for them to run away and not look back, as fast as she and Chance could go. Chance was able to keep her calm after the first text, but when they saw someone buy the information, she became even more frantic and desperately wanted to run. Chance knew she wouldn't stay put for long. He understood that the woman he was in love with was a runner. If she felt either one of them were in danger, she would run and never stop running, to save both their lives. His only option was to get to Freddy and find out what he knew about everything. However, Chance already believed he knew who was selling the information and who was buying it. Still, he wanted Freddy to confirm it.

Leontii, Boris, and Igor sat in the penthouse office suite

of the Emerald Coast Casino, trying to figure out what they needed to do next. Leontii knew he had to deliver Chance Hardway to the Romano family. He was using the thumb drive that held the video of Morgan killing Juan Muñoz to draw the man out, but he wasn't confident it would work. He needed a backup plan.

"What if our plan fails to draw Hardway out?" Leontii asked of his two men.

"We could offer a bounty to anyone who could tell us where Hardway is," Igor suggested.

"How?"

"We use the Underground again," Igor answered flatly.

"This could get us a lot of exposure. The police monitor the Underground messages just like everyone else. We've already sold information to the Muñoz Cartel, and now we're offering a bounty for Hardway. This could bring more than local cops to our front door." Boris said, reminding the others.

"I know, but we must protect the family. We don't want a war with Edward Romano. If we don't deliver Hardway, then it could come to that. Besides, we don't know who killed our own people and if they have access to our accounts. We have to take the risk with the Underground," Leontii explained.

"How much?" Igor asked as he prepared the text message.

"Two hundred and fifty thousand," Leontii answered as he walked to his desk.

Boris looked at his boss but didn't say anything. He was allowing the man to dig his own grave.

"What the fuck!" Freddy said when he saw the next text come through. He was sitting in the dining room, monitoring the Underground's website and listening to show tunes, when he saw the latest text.

"What's wrong?" Candi asked from the kitchen.

"Someone's offering a bounty on Chance. They want to know where he can be found."

Candi walked in and looked over the big man's shoulder at the computer screen. "Two hundred and fifty thousand dollars! Do you know where he is?"

"No, I don't. No one knows where he is or where he lives. The man's done a good job of keeping his information private," Freddy answered unconvincingly. He found out where Chance lived months ago but never shared the information with anyone. Freddy knew it was better to have the former Green Beret as a friend rather than an enemy.

"That's too bad," Candi remarked as she walked toward the front door.

"Where're you going?"

"Out shopping. Would you like to go?"

"No," Freddy quickly answered. He hated shopping, and he hated spending money more, which was what Candi would want him to do if he went with her.

"Okay, I'll see you later. Maybe I'll bring you some dinner when I come back."

Candi walked out before Freddy could say anything else. When she got to her car, she got in and backed out of the driveway. As she drove down the road, she reached over to open the glove box and took out her other cell phone. Candi dialed the number from memory and waited for her friend to answer.

Rebecca Hicks was sitting at the bar of the Show and Go. The Show and Go was a private swingers' club that couples paid to be a member of, in the hopes of finding another swinger couple. Rebecca had been hired to get photos of a married man who frequented the establishment with his mistress. She was about to enjoy a shot of whiskey when her phone vibrated in her pocket.

"What," Rebecca said, answering the call.

"It's me."

"I know, Candi. It's called caller ID." Rebecca shook her head in frustration and threw the whiskey back.

"Oh, yeah. Someone's offering a lot of money for Chance Hardway."

"I know. I got the text like everyone else did. No one knows where he is. I tried, but he found the tracking device on his truck." Rebecca motioned the bartender to pour her another one.

"If I knew someone who knew where he lived, and I told you, would you split the two hundred and fifty thousand with me?" Candi asked.

"Yeah. An eighty-twenty split."

"Eighty for me and twenty for you?" Candi asked.

"No, eighty for me and twenty for you. I'm the one who must get the information out of this person. That's something that could get dirty."

"I can't do that. I'll get someone else to do it," Candi replied and got ready to end the call.

"No, wait. What's your offer?" Rebecca asked. Her hard-nosed approach wasn't going to work with a clueless girl like Candi.

"I want a fifty-fifty split," Candi replied.

Rebecca threw the second shot back. "Fine."

Boris left the suite and made his way through the casino toward the parking garage. While on his way, he took out his phone and made a call. Boris had been waiting for the right time to get the second part of his plan going, and now seemed to be the right time to do it.

"Pavel, call Maxim, and the two of you get to Las Vegas and let me know when you get here. Stay out of sight," Boris ordered and then ended the call without allowing Pavel to respond. When he got to his car, he got inside and drove out of the parking garage. As he drove through the city, he imagined being the Gorky's top man. Boris Yelchin was going to get what he deserved to have. If he didn't, he would replace the entire Gorky organization with the Yelchin organization. Boris had made the Bratva a lot of money, but over the years, Boris had grown tired of being overlooked by Ivan Gorky. He kept quiet when other people were promoted over him. Most recently Boris expected to be the next brigadier, but Ivan selected Leontii over him, and that was the last straw.

Boris had thought everything through carefully after seeing that someone was looking for Sava and Luca a while ago. After rushing to Las Vegas, he found both Sava and Luca at their apartment. The two men had stolen a car near a hiking trail and drove back to their place after Hardway left them in the desert. The men were beaten, and they had a score to settle with the man who had done the beating. Boris learned that Hardway had taken them to the desert, beaten them, and left them there in revenge for what they had done to his girlfriend, Morgan. He knew a man like Hardway wouldn't stop until he got to everyone involved, including him.

That day, Boris lied to Sava and Luca by telling them the Bratva had already captured Hardway right before his arrival. He told the two men that they had Igor take Hardway to the desert and they were waiting for Sava and Luca to arrive. Both Sava and Luca got into Boris's car without a second thought. Boris drove them back out to the desert where the two men hoped to settle the score with Chance Hardway. When the three men were alone, Boris executed both of his fellow Bratva and left them there, dead and naked.

The killing of Anton, the accountant, was not part of Boris's plan. Still, after it happened, Boris made sure everything else would be done how he expected, including having Vlad and Vasily killed by their own men. Boris had promised both Pavel and Maxim high-ranking positions under his command if the two of them followed his orders to the letter. He made sure Chance Hardway took the blame for the murders. Now, he needed to make sure that Leontii was viewed as a failure by the Gorky family, and killed.

As Boris drove through the city, he listened to an old Russian ballad about World War II and imagined how things would be under his command. He would get what he deserved or die trying.

Ricky had gotten to the storage building where he, Bobby, and the others had planned the failed hit at the federal courthouse. Bobby had selected the meeting spot and insisted on meeting there. Ricky suggested somewhere else. He was worried the feds and the local cops were chasing down every possible lead from the shooting, which could come back to the storage building. Bobby was nervous and demanded they meet there. He wasn't comfortable going anywhere else that he wasn't already familiar with within the city of Las Vegas.

It was an hour after Ricky arrived when he finally heard someone driving into the building. He knew something needed to be done, and he had already made his mind up before Bobby arrived. Ricky was sitting behind the desk in the office when Bobby walked in.

"Do you know where we can find Hardway?" Bobby asked after stepping into the office. He stood in front of the desk with his pistol handle sticking out the front of his pants.

"No, I don't," Ricky answered as he stood and looked the man over. He could tell Bobby was on edge. If there was any question about what needed to be done before Bobby arrived, it was gone now.

"How can we find him?" Bobby asked and started pacing back and forth.

"For a man who does our type of work, you seem to be nervous. You knew the risk when you got involved. You were here when we discussed the plan. You could have left anytime you wanted," Ricky said to remind the man and then sat back down. "Besides, I know what to do about it." Ricky leaned forward and used the desk to conceal his hand as he drew his pistol from his waistline.

"You should be nervous too! More than a few dead feds are lying in the morgue because of us, and now their friends are looking for the people responsible. The only thing that can lead them to us is Chance Hardway, and I want to know what you've got planned," Bobby demanded and slowly moved his hand toward his own gun.

"Actually, the only thing that can lead them to us is you," Ricky declared as he pushed himself back from the desk while raising the pistol in Bobby's direction.

Bobby quickly pulled his own gun. The men started shooting at each other, filling the room with the sound of gunfire and smoke. Ricky was hit in the left shoulder. He grimaced in pain after his gun emptied. He then watched his fellow operator drop sluggishly to his knees.

Bobby felt as though the room was spinning. He tilted his head upward and then fell back onto the floor.

Ricky sat in the office chair for a second and then walked to the dead man, where he stood over his body. He looked down at Bobby for a moment and walked out of the office. Chance Hardway had nothing on him, nor could he tie him to anything. Once he retrieved his money, he would make Las Vegas a memory.

Chance was careful after he left his place. The drive to Freddy's took longer than usual. Along the route, Chance drove through various neighborhoods, making the standard right turns to see if anyone was following him. When he was on the interstate, he took different exits. He would immediately get back onto the interstate, continuing to check his mirrors, looking for a possible tail. About an hour later, he pulled into Freddy's driveway just as Candi returned from an apparent shopping trip. Chance got out of his truck, nodded at Candi, and started for the front porch. When he was about to knock on the door, it suddenly opened.

"Quick, get in here!" Freddy ordered. He then saw Candi walking up the sidewalk behind Chance.

"Okay," Chance replied and made his way past Freddy's large frame.

"What's going on? Who's that?" Candi asked and pointed inside toward Chance.

"It's no one, honey," Freddy answered.

"No one." she repeated in frustration as she put her hand on her waist. She was upset with Freddy for blowing her off.

"Candi, you can't be here right now. Go get us some food, and I'll talk to you when you get back," Freddy stated and abruptly shut the door.

Candi knew who the man was, and now she was angry that Freddy didn't trust her and had dismissed her so rudely. She quickly got over it when she remembered the bounty on Chance Hardway. Candi wanted to claim it right then but knew she could not. If she answered the Underground's ad, Freddy would realize it was her. The best thing for her to do was call Rebecca and tell her where Chance Hardway could be found. Half of two hundred and fifty thousand dollars was better than losing her sugar daddy, and that was precisely what would happen if she claimed the bounty herself.

When she got back to her car, Candi took her other cell phone out of the glove box once more and called Rebecca.

Freddy sat at the head of the dining room table. "Have a seat," Freddy said excitedly.

"Who's looking for Morgan and me?" Chance asked without hesitating.

"Well, the word on the street is—"

"Stop! I know you're the Underground. I've known about it for a while now. No one knows more than you about everyone and everything in Las Vegas, and there's only one way that you could get all that information. Now, tell me what you know!" Chance demanded and moved closer to the man. He wasn't in the mood to play games. He needed to know what Freddy knew, and he needed to know now.

"I... I..." Freddy stammered as he tried to think of something to say.

"Look, getting Junior back here, the thumb drive in Chicago, and the signature on the real estate papers in Los Angeles were for someone who paid you. I want to know who it was!" Chance demanded, leaning closer to the large man in a hostile manner. Chance liked Freddy, but he knew he might have to pressure him a little to get what he needed.

"Okay, someone did pay me for two of the jobs, but it didn't start out that way. Eddie's bail skip was a real deal, but after you went there and killed the accountant, someone reached out to me through the Underground's email, asking if I could get the other stuff done."

"Who was it?"

"I don't know, and that's the truth," Freddy confessed and sat there a moment. "There is something else you should know."

"What?"

"The person who needed the jobs done asked for you specifically."

"Why?"

"Look, you're known for getting things done. At the time,

I just thought they had heard of you and your reputation," Freddy explained, moving his hands around in the air as he did so. The man couldn't seem to speak without the use of his hands. "But…"

"But what, Freddy?"

"I think someone is setting you up, and they have been since I got the first email."

"Who is it?"

"Me," Freddy sadly confessed.

"You?"

"Well, I mean, I wasn't in on it, but I did help without knowing what this guy was up to," Freddy quickly clarified when he saw Chance start to get angry.

"Tell me everything you know."

"All right. When you wanted me to get the information on the men who hurt Morgan, I used other sources for it. I wasn't going to put it out through the Underground, especially after you killed Sava and Luca, and—"

"Okay, let's get a few things straight. I didn't kill the accountant. The Romano family did. Well, I think the men were part of the Romano family. Anyway, I didn't kill Sava and Luca either. I don't know who killed them," Chance explained and waited for Freddy to say something.

The large man took a minute to think about what Chance had said. "That could only mean one thing." Freddy rested his chin on his hand.

"What?"

"Someone's making a move," Freddy answered.

"Who?"

"Someone in the Gorky organization, I think."

Rebecca was still at the Show and Go when she received the second call from Candi. It was the break she needed. The man

Rebecca was waiting for still hadn't arrived with his mistress, and Rebecca needed to make some money. After getting off the phone with Candi, Rebecca responded to the text from the Underground concerning Chance Hardway. Rebecca had disliked Chance ever since she met him in a bar to deliver Senator Ken Davenport's video. The video was worth a lot more than what she was paid, and all she wanted to do was renegotiate the deal. Chance wasn't having any part of it that day, and he took the video from her by force.

Putting his hands on me was a big mistake, Rebecca thought to herself as she waited for a response from the person who was buying the information she was selling.

Leontii retrieved his phone from his pocket and read the text message he had just received. He smiled when he read the words. Someone was ready to provide the location of Chance Hardway.

"What is it?" Igor asked.

"I think we're about to get our hands on Chance Hardway."

"Good, then war with the Romano family can be avoided. We'll hand him over to them and let them kill him," Igor happily suggested.

"Yes, we will," Leontii replied.

Chance was still waiting for Freddy to continue when the computer on the table chimed. Freddy turned the screen back on and read the new text message. Chance waited for him to say something more, but the large man only looked at Chance.

"What is it now?" Chance asked.

"Someone is selling the information on you," Freddy answered reluctantly.

"How and who?"

"I recognize the number," Freddy stated.

"Who is it?"

"Rebecca Hicks."

"Great! How does she know how to find me?" Chance asked out loud without expecting an answer.

"I don't know."

"Tell me what you were about to tell me, Freddy."

"I think someone is making a move on the Gorky family."

"What makes you think that?" Chance asked as he walked around the table and peeked out the window at the street in front of Freddy's house. He needed to be cautious.

"Well, you didn't kill Sava and Luca, but you were looking for them, to get revenge for what they did to Morgan. If that information got out to the right person, then all they had to do was put things into motion so you'd take the fall for killing the others. Now, all you need to do is find out who would benefit from it all," Freddy explained.

"It has to be the person who sent the email, but we don't know who that is." Chance sat back down in the chair next to Freddy.

"Not yet, we don't," Freddy replied.

"How does Morgan fit into all of this? Why come after her now?" Chance asked.

"Someone is after her to get to you. If you're busy protecting her, you're an easier target."

Chance sat there trying to work things out in his head, but Freddy's computer chimed once more. Freddy looked at the screen and then slowly turned around toward Chance. He just stared at the man who now had a new two-million-open kill bounty on his head.

CHAPTER 13
THE TWO-MILLION-
DOLLAR MAN

Boris pulled off the road into a gas station parking lot when he read someone had located Chance Hardway and offered to sell the man's location to Leontii. He ran numerous scenarios through his mind before concluding that Chance Hardway needed to die. If Hardway were captured and questioned by Ivan or Leontii, then he would deny killing the others. Hardway would also deny knowing anything about the thumb drives with the bank accounts and passwords taken from Anton. In Boris's mind, there was only one thing left to do, which was to outbid Leontii to make sure Hardway would never live to be questioned. Besides, the money on the thumb drives would soon be his.

Boris already had the banks' names where the Gorky's money was located, and the names of where it was going next. He had obtained Anton's method of moving money after he got the accountant drunk one night a few months ago. That night, as Anton slept, Boris's personal computer hacker inserted a Botnet, a spy malware that collected information on the keystrokes of the drunken man's laptop. The hacker's malware was only partially successful in getting the passwords. Since Anton's death, Boris had moved about ten million dollars from Anton's personal accounts and the Gorky's accounts into his own bank accounts. Still there was more to get, if Boris's hacker could get the other passwords and account numbers that Anton had created the night he was killed. Boris had his computer hacker working day and night searching for and deciphering the other passwords and bank accounts that belonged to the Gorky family. If Boris was successful in getting all the money, he could turn it over to Ivan Gorky, who would be very pleased with him. The leader of the Bratva would have to promote him. If he did not, then Boris would keep it all and start his own organization, while eliminating the old one at the same time, which included killing Ivan and his loyal followers.

After a few minutes of deliberation, he decided to spend some of the ten million dollars by offering a two-million-dollar, open-kill contract on Chance Hardway.

Morgan was sitting in the RV, getting more and more nervous by the minute, and when the bounties came in on Chance, she rushed into the bedroom and started packing their stuff. It was time to leave Las Vegas. Where the two of them would go, she didn't know, but anywhere was safer than where they were. She was busy packing things when she heard her phone ringing in the living room. Morgan dropped the bag she had in her hand and ran to answer it.

"Chance?" Morgan said into the receiver without looking at the caller ID first.

"No, but if you could tell me where he is, I promise I won't kill him," Leontii offered.

"And me, what do you promise will happen to me?" Morgan asked.

"Morgan, there's nothing I can do for you now. The Muñoz Cartel is after you."

"Yes, I know, and I wonder who put them onto me?" Morgan asked rhetorically.

"Something is going on you're not aware of. Unfortunately, that something is worth a lot more than you," Leontii confessed.

"Like what?"

"Like a thumb drive."

Morgan remembered the thumb drives she saw Chance holding the other night. Both were still lying in the glass dish in the living room. She walked over and picked them up.

"What's on it?" Morgan asked calmly, not knowing which one he was referring to.

"Millions. Do you know where it is? It could buy you out of your situation."

"No, I don't. Besides, there's no way I would ever trust you if I did. You hurt me, and I would never do anything that helped you in the slightest."

"Is that why you had Hardway kill my men? Am I next on his list?" Leontii asked, but Morgan didn't answer.

After a brief pause, she ended the call and stood there holding the thumb drives. She knew she needed to put them somewhere safe.

Leontii didn't expect Morgan to answer him. He just wanted to keep her on the phone.

"Do you know her location?" Leontii asked.

"Yeah, she's near the strip in an old area of Las Vegas. Here's the address," Ben answered and collected his computer equipment. Ben Smith was hired by the Russian boss to trace a phone call. After he got the other person's location, he handed the address to his employer and started for the door.

"Do you know anyone who can recover passwords?" Leontii asked before the hacker walked out.

"No, I just do what I do and leave the other stuff alone."

"That's too bad. I need someone, and I'll pay them very well if they can get what I need."

"I'll check around, and if I find someone, I'll be sure to send them your way," Ben replied and walked out of the office suite. He didn't want anything else to do with the Russian Mafia.

Rebecca and her men sat in her car a few houses down the street from Freddy's place. She was only able to find two other hired guns to help her with getting Chance. She and the two men were getting impatient waiting for Hardway to come out. They knew it wouldn't be easy grabbing the experienced operator, but the money being offered was well worth the risk.

"What's he doing in there?" the man sitting in the back seat asked.

"How am I supposed to know? All I know is he's inside," Rebecca replied in a sarcastic tone. The man sitting behind her had made a few comments on the way over that made Rebecca question his qualifications, but she decided that it was too late to replace him now. He would have to do. She started to change the station on the radio when she heard another text come through. She picked up her phone and looked at the message from the Underground. "We're not going to have to grab him." Rebecca opened the driver's door. She quickly got out and walked to the rear of the car to open the trunk. The two men sitting in the car got out and joined her.

"Take these and quickly get back in the car," Rebecca ordered as she handed one man an AR-15 and the other a shotgun.

"I thought we were just grabbing this guy. Why the heavy equipment?" one of the gunmen asked.

"His bounty just changed to two million and I plan on collecting it," Rebecca announced and quickly got back inside the car.

"So now we're going to get paid two million dollars to just grab this guy?" the gunman in the passenger seat, holding the AR-15, asked suspiciously.

"No, a new bounty just came out. Hardway's been greenlit," Rebecca explained as she checked her 9 mm, opened the center console, and grabbed three more loaded magazines.

"What's the plan?" the gunman in the back asked, not knowing what it meant to be greenlit.

"We take him at an intersection. I'll pull up next to him. The two of you get out quickly and let him have it. I'll stand back, ready to go when it's done," Rebecca answered. She grabbed her phone and responded to the text.

Chance was still sitting in Freddy's house when countless text messages started coming in through the Underground. Freddy read them as fast as he could, while Chance watched the large man rock back and forth.

"What's going on, Freddy?" Chance asked.

"Someone says they'll do it and have it done in the next hour," Freddy answered nervously.

"What else is happening? What's with all the messages?"

"People all over are offering to buy any information that leads them to you," Freddy explained and then shut the computer off.

"I got to get Morgan and get her out of here," Chance stated and started for the door.

"Wait!" Freddy yelled. He ran into the living room and opened a safe he kept hidden in the coffee table.

Chance stood still, not knowing what the man was doing.

"Here, take this and don't tell anyone where you're going.

I don't want to know either," Freddy said as he stuffed a large envelope with cash and then handed it to Chance.

"What's this?" Chance asked as he held the thick envelope.

"I don't know, a bonus… or an advance maybe. Call it whatever you want. Just take it!"

"Why?"

"I don't know. Just go get Morgan, and the two of you find someplace safe. Stay off your phones, away from cameras and anything that can be used to track you digitally. I'll slow down the Underground."

"Thanks, Freddy," Chance replied and hurried out the door.

Ricky pulled up to the storage facility's entrance gate, and after entering his code, the gate slowly opened. When he pulled his arm back inside, he was immediately reminded of the bullet hole in his shoulder. He closed his eyes and waited until the pain went away. He then drove over to storage unit 4200. Ricky figured things were too hot for him and he needed to get out of town soon, but he wasn't leaving without his money. He looked around the area before reaching down and grabbing the lock, but he found it cut. He closed his eyes, took a deep breath, and lifted the heavy door.

"Shit!" Ricky yelled as he looked at his empty storage unit. His money was gone. The injured man climbed back into his car and scrolled through the contacts in his cell phone. He soon found the name he was looking for and called her.

"Hello," Lynn said when she answered the call.

"Where's my money?" Ricky asked.

"Well, it wasn't really yours, was it?"

"I'm going to find you, and you'll be sorry when I do."

"You'll try, but I don't think you'll be able to find me," Lynn stated and ended the call.

Ricky closed his eyes. After a few minutes, he drove out the gate and headed for the interstate. He turned on the radio, grabbed his phone, and pulled up the tracking app. He smiled when he saw the red light flashing on the map somewhere over the Pacific Ocean. He recalled a previous conversation he and Lynn had in a hotel room. During pillow talk between the two, Lynn told Ricky she had family in Hawaii and desperately wanted to move there.

"Hawaii, I always wanted to visit the islands," Ricky said and turned the music up.

Chance headed back to his place in a hurry. He decided to take Freddy up on his advice to get himself and Morgan out of Las Vegas. On his drive back, Chance took all the same precautions he had taken earlier. He exited the interstate and drove through neighborhoods making consecutive right turns. When he exited onto Sahara Avenue, he turned left onto Rancho Drive. It was there, at the intersection, where he observed the dark-blue sedan once more. The driver had followed him from the interstate through the intersection onto Rancho Drive. Chance had noticed the car earlier when he exited the interstate, and again, he saw it behind him when he got back on.

The word was out on the street. Everyone in Sin City was looking for Chance Hardway. When Santiago saw the custom pickup cruising through the intersection, he grabbed his phone. He scrolled through his text messages, and after a few seconds, he found the number he was looking for. Santiago presented himself to others as a Colombian-born national who immigrated to the United States with his family when he was ten years old, but Santiago Perez was much more than that.

"Chance Hardway, the two-million-dollar man," Santiago said to himself as he dialed the number and waited for the man to answer. "Hardway's in the area of Sahara and Rancho, heading south. I'll keep him in sight until you get here."

Santiago got off the phone and began following the custom pickup.

Rebecca and her two accomplices had followed Hardway all the way from Freddy's place. She tried to use the tailing techniques she had read about online. She thought she was doing a good job.

"When are we going to do it?" the gunman in the back asked as he checked his weapon once more.

"When he stops again, we do it," Rebecca stated. She was nervous, but nothing was going to stop her from collecting on the bounty.

Chance watched in his rearview mirror as the blue sedan followed him onto Kings Drive. There was no denying it. He had a tail, and he was sure that whoever it was, they were out to collect on the two-million bounty. He reached over and grabbed the pistol he had at the ready on the seat next to him. Slowly, Chance pulled to a stop at the red light at Teddy Drive and watched the sedan as it approached. He placed his hand on the door handle. He prepared to perform a high-risk maneuver that he hoped would give him a tactical advantage. As the sedan got closer, Chance got ready.

He was about to exit the truck when two Las Vegas Metro Police cruisers came flying into the intersection with their lights and sirens blaring and blocking his path. Chance laid the pistol on the floorboard, then placed his hands in the air and watched in the rearview mirror. The sedan made a U-turn in the roadway and left the area in the opposite direction.

Morgan paced back and forth in the RV, waiting for Chance. He had texted her an hour ago, telling her he was on his way back and that she needed to pack their stuff so they could leave

Las Vegas. She was happy for the moment but was getting restless. She decided to call Chance to see where he was, just as she heard someone coming up to the RV. She dropped her phone onto the counter and ran for the door.

"Chance!" Morgan yelled excitedly, but her excitement quickly waned when she saw Igor standing there with two other men. Behind them, sitting in the back seat of his luxury car, was Leontii. Morgan tried to shut the door, but it was no use. Igor grabbed it and forced his way inside. Morgan rushed toward the kitchen, but Igor grabbed her by the hair and dragged her outside. She fought as much as she could, but it was no use. The other two men grabbed her by the arms and held her up. Leontii got out of the car and looked at the woman while Igor walked back inside the RV.

Leontii grabbed her by the hair and tilted her head back. "Where's your boyfriend?"

"I don't know."

"He's not here. All their stuff is packed, and it looks like she's been texting Hardway," Igor announced as he walked back outside, holding Morgan's phone in his hand.

"That's too bad," the Russian boss said and released his grip on Morgan. He started back toward the car. "Teach her a small lesson. Make sure she's quiet when you put her in the trunk and then send Hardway a picture of her."

Igor placed the phone in his pocket, stood in front of Morgan, and smiled. She started to cry out loud when she saw Igor reaching back with a closed fist. She began to beg, knowing what was about to happen.

"No, please..."

Chance did not move. He just waited as the uniformed officers approached his car with their weapons drawn. He didn't know what to expect, but whatever it was, it wasn't good.

"Driver, slowly open the door and step out with your hands in the air," one of the officers ordered.

Chance did as he was told and got out of the truck. He was quickly handcuffed, searched, and placed into the back seat of one of the cruisers. He watched as they searched his truck. He still didn't know what they had on him or why they had stopped him. He was still watching them when someone walked up and knocked on the side window. Chance turned and looked at the familiar man standing next to the door. Detective Santiago Perez, an old acquaintance from Metro, opened the door and motioned for Chance to get out of the car.

"I always knew you'd end up in the backseat of a police car," Santiago stated as he turned Chance around and removed the handcuffs. Santiago had met Chance when he worked for Metro, but the two never really got along.

"What's going on?" Chance asked after he turned back around and faced Santiago.

"I don't know, but I think he may," Santiago suggested and pointed toward an unmarked car pulling up to them. The two men watched as the driver's door opened and a slow-moving Sergeant Parker Denton got out. Parker wore a sweatsuit, had one arm in a sling, and used a cane to walk toward the two men.

"I'm supposed to be at home healing," Parker declared.

"Why aren't you?" Chance asked.

"I'll give you two million guesses why I'm not," Parker stated and waited for Chance to say something.

"Don't worry about it. I can handle it. I'm leaving town just as soon as I get back to Morgan," Chance confessed and started to walk back toward his truck.

"Then what?" Parker asked.

"I don't know. I'm kind of winging it right now." Chance watched as one of the uniformed officers walked by him, carrying his gun and Freddy's money. "I'm going to need all of that!" Chance declared and started back toward Parker, who had taken possession of the items from the officer.

"I'll decide if you need these or not," Parker said in response.

Santiago stepped in front of Chance, blocking his path to Parker. Chance stopped just short of the man. He knew Santiago's reputation for being quick with his hands, but Chance wasn't worried. He would do what was necessary to make sure he got back to Morgan.

"Step back!" Santiago ordered and then used both hands to push Chance backward.

Chance wasn't having it. He went at Santiago and pushed him back, sending the man to the ground. The other officers moved toward Chance while Santiago quickly got back to his feet.

"Everyone, stop it!" Parker ordered. He walked to Chance and handed him the gun and the money. "You need to let me help you."

"Help! Help how?"

"Santiago has a man in the Muñoz Cartel. His guy says the cartel is coming for Morgan," Parker explained.

"I already know. There's nothing you or the asshole next to you can do about it," Chance argued and started back to his truck again.

"I can put her into witness protection. She's got information on the Russian Mafia and maybe something on the Muñoz Cartel. We can protect her, and you," Parker offered as he hobbled to catch up with his old friend.

"I saw how witness protection worked out for the marshals outside the federal courthouse. If I remember right, it was me who stopped them from killing the witnesses and you. I'll bet on me over you and your people any day," Chance proclaimed before climbing back into his truck and speeding away, leaving Parker and the others standing in the intersection.

Chance was getting anxious. He had an overwhelming feeling that something was wrong. He needed to get back to Morgan. When his phone chimed, he picked it up and saw a text from her. The only problem was someone else had sent it, along with a photo of Morgan lying on the ground in front of the RV.

"Damn it!"

CHAPTER 14
A FATHER'S REVENGE

Hector Muñoz sat in the back seat with his eyes closed, listening to the sounds of jazz playing through the multiple speakers that surrounded him in the luxury limousine. He seldom traveled outside of Colombia, but this trip was a special one. Hector was paying someone to deliver the person responsible for his son's murder. He had been waiting for years to get his revenge, and now he was about to get it. Hector had spent the past few days planning what he was going to do to the person who killed his only son. He smiled as he fantasized about killing the woman he saw in the video. He imagined her begging him to kill her to end the torture he would inflict on her.

"Papá, it's time for your medicine," Mariana said as she reached out with a bottle of water in one hand and a pill in the other.

"No, not now, Mariana," Hector declined while shaking his hand back and forth in front of her.

"Yes, Papá. You must take it. It's for your heart."

"I know, but my heart has been broken for a very long time, and no medicine can repair it," Hector confessed.

"I know, Papá, but you must take it. Here, no more

arguing." Mariana grabbed her father's hands and placed the water bottle in one and the pill in the other. "Now, put it in your mouth and swallow it," Mariana stated and watched her father intently until he did as she said.

"Is everything ready?" Hector asked.

"Yes, I've made arrangements to stay in one of our private houses far from the Strip. I have our people in place. Now, we're just waiting for the contact to call so that we can make arrangements for the package to be delivered," Mariana explained and then answered her phone that was ringing.

Hector watched and listened as his daughter conducted the Muñoz family business over the phone. Mariana had taken on the responsibility that was supposed to have been passed to Juan. Since Hector's heart attack last year and Juan's murder before that, Mariana had stepped in and taken over everything. The only heir to the Muñoz fortune was thirty-five years old, smart, beautiful, and ruthless. She had dark-green eyes, and the cartel soldiers believed she could see into a man's soul. It was rumored she was a bruja, a witch who had the power to control the hearts and minds of men. She was already being referred to as *La Capitana Bruja de Colombia*. The Witch Captain of Colombia had ordered the killing of countless police informants, traitors, enemies, and others who refused to cooperate or betray the Muñoz Cartel. Now, she was helping her father to avenge Juan's murder.

"You've done well with our family's business, Mariana. You make me proud," Hector confessed after his daughter ended the call. Still, he didn't think she would be a proper heir to take over the cartel.

"Thank you, Papá."

"Soon, we will avenge your brother's death. I will hold his killer's head in my hands!" Hector clenched his fist tightly.

"Yes, Papá," Mariana responded. She knew her brother was a killer who had taken the lives of countless women in both Colombia and the United States. She also knew Juan had inherited his taste for raping and killing women from his father. In Mariana's opinion, the woman she and her father saw in the video killing Juan did so in self-defense, but that didn't matter to her father. Hector had to seek revenge for his son's murder. If he didn't, and that information got out to his enemies, it would be viewed as a sign of weakness. Weaknesses encouraged takeovers and wars among Colombian cartels. Mariana had to do whatever was necessary to make sure the Muñoz cartel was forever strong in the eyes of their enemies.

Chance wasted no time in getting back to his place, only to find the keypad to the gate disabled and the gate sitting wide open. Instead of driving through the open gate, he got out and slowly made his way around the backside of his building with his gun in hand, cautiously looking around. Behind a large air compressor, he dropped to a knee and took out his phone. He called Morgan, but all it did was ring until it went to her voicemail. He didn't expect her to answer, but he had hoped to hear the phone ringing from somewhere inside the building. After a few attempts, Chance placed the phone back into his pocket and came around to the left side of the metal building. He made his way toward the front, making sure he stayed close to the wall as he did so.

Rebecca had successfully followed Chance. When he left the intersection, he was in a hurry. He had not taken any side roads, nor did he leave the interstate until he reached the exit that brought him to this location. Rebecca thought the entire area appeared to have been an industrial business district many years ago. Now, it was nothing more than a few empty, decaying buildings. When she saw Chance's truck parked in front of the open gate, she drove down the street and parked behind an old factory, then ordered the hired gunmen out of the car.

"You go through the main gate, and you come around the back with me," she instructed.

"What if I see him?" the man who had been sitting in the back seat asked.

"Use that gun and kill him. He's worth two million bucks," Rebecca explained with a surprised look on her face. She watched as the man started for the gate. "What did he think we were going to do? I think we'll be splitting the bounty between the two of us after this is all done."

"Yeah, he's an odd one, odd enough to maybe talk to people after this is over," Axel, the other gunman, suggested. Ax, as he liked to be called, was an experienced killer, although he had no professional training as one. It was the impoverished streets of Miami that served as his training grounds. Under the hot Florida sun, he hired himself out as a contract killer and was successful at it until he missed a mark a few months ago. Ax had to leave Miami or be killed himself, and he landed in Las Vegas answering ads like the one Rebecca had placed.

"Sounds like you and I will be the only two walking out of here when this is over. A fifty-fifty split is better than a third," Rebecca stated, even though she had already decided to kill both men when it was over. She was the type of woman who believed the best way to keep a secret was to take it with you to the grave and allow others to do the same.

"It's a deal," Ax replied.

Chance cautiously continued on his way in the hopes of finding Morgan. He quietly entered the main building through a concealed door he had cut into the side when he first began converting the old factory. On the inside, the concealed door was hidden behind a large and old hollowed-out upright freezer. He cracked the door open, waited, and listened for anyone inside. When he didn't hear anything, he opened the door and stepped onto the concrete pad. He held his gun at the ready. He then made his way toward the front of his RV, where he could get closer to the front without anyone inside seeing his approach.

Rebecca and Ax had taken the same path as Chance but didn't know it. The two of them tried to look inside the building through the windows but found them painted over with black paint.

"Where is he?" Rebecca asked.

"I don't know. He had to have a reason to park out front. I mean, why wouldn't he just drive through the main gate?"

"I don't know. Keep moving toward the front of the building. Maybe he went inside."

The gunman from the back seat was not trained in military tactics. His name was Willard, and he had lied about his skills with the hope of getting some fast cash. Now, he found himself entirely out of his environment, not knowing what to do if he saw the man they were supposed to kill. The shotgun he carried felt awkward in his hands. He knew how to use it, but he didn't think he was ready to kill someone.

"Damn, all I needed was a few thousand dollars to pay my bookie. What am I doing here?" Willard asked himself as he moved toward the open garage. He looked around cautiously as he got closer. He was scared and out of place. More than once, he thought about running away. Still, the opportunity for a big payday kept him walking forward into the building.

Chance reached up and placed his hand on the doorknob of the RV. He was about to open it when he heard someone coming up behind him through the open garage. He quickly turned around and discovered a man walking inside, carrying a shotgun.

Willard was caught off guard. He looked at Chance, and out of fear and pure adrenaline, he gripped the shotgun tighter.

"Don't do it!" Chance ordered, but it was no use. His words fell upon deaf ears.

Willard raised his shotgun toward his target and prematurely fired one round, hitting the concrete floor in front of him.

Without hesitation, Chance placed two rounds into the man's chest, dropping him to the ground.

Willard thought about his mom, brother, and girlfriend as he lay there on the cool cement floor while his blood pooled around his dying body. Willard didn't know the man he was there to kill, but now, that man stood over him as he took his final breath.

Chance knelt and felt for a pulse in the gunman's neck, but there wasn't one. He then looked around the area outside near the open garage but didn't see anyone else milling around.

When Rebecca and her accomplice heard the shots, they dropped to the ground and waited at the ready.

"Do you think our guy got him?" Ax asked.

"Those didn't sound like shotgun rounds to me," Rebecca answered.

Edward Romano Sr. sat in the Galleria Hotel and Casino's luxury suite, impatiently waiting for a phone call from Leontii. Usually, when the Mafia boss was in Las Vegas for pleasure, he stayed in the beautiful hotel enjoying late-night strolls through the various galleries, admiring the works of art on display. Unfortunately, Edward wasn't in Las Vegas for pleasure. He was there for business.

The business he was there for was getting delayed, and he was growing impatient with every passing hour. He wanted the name of the person responsible for his son's murder, and he wanted it yesterday. Rico, his top man and nephew, had been in and out of the suite. Rico reported back to his uncle on anything and everything happening back in Philly. Since

Junior's death, Edward had ignored important business back home, and Rico knew others were starting to notice. He made every attempt to keep things moving as if nothing had changed, but people were talking. He believed that if the boss didn't get back to business as usual, someone could make a move on the Romano Family.

"What is it? Has the Russian called?" Edward asked angrily when Rico entered the room.

"No, not yet."

"Fucking Russians! Leontii is middle management. Get me in contact with Ivan Gorky!" Edward yelled and walked to the large window overlooking the strip.

"Uncle, I just got off the phone. Some of our payments are not being made in Philly," Rico said, informing the boss that things were not as they should be in his absence.

"I don't care about Philly right now. I want my son's killer!"

"Yes, right away," Rico said as he walked out of the suite. He knew trying to reason with his uncle was of no use. The business in Philly would be left to him, a middle manager, to take care of.

Chance left the man lying on the ground and started back toward his RV. When he got to the door, he eased it open with one hand and kept his gun ready in the other. As he stepped inside, he was cautious. There was no way of knowing who or what was waiting for him.

Rebecca and Ax stood back up and once again made their way toward the front of the metal building. When they reached the open garage, Rebecca signaled for Ax to enter first. Ax shook his head and made his way inside. Once he was inside, Ax saw Willard lying on the ground in a pool of blood. He stepped past the dead man and took cover behind an old car engine being supported by a lift. He then signaled for Rebecca to come inside.

Chance moved through his RV, looking for any possible accomplices of the man he had just killed. When he was sure he was alone, he looked at all of his personal belongings strewn around in the RV.

"Someone was looking for something," he whispered.

Rebecca quietly stepped past Axel as she made her way closer to the RV. She kept her pistol aimed at the front door. Rebecca was scared, but she didn't show it. She just bit her lip and pressed forward.

Ax kept the butt of the AR-15 snug against his shoulder, covering Rebecca. He smiled when he realized the possibility of taking out both the target and Rebecca if the situation presented itself.

Chance looked at everything lying about on the floor, and he kicked his belongings aside as he made his way toward the kitchen. He didn't understand what he could possibly have that someone else wanted, other than Morgan. When he got to the kitchen, he looked down, and next to the sink cabinet was his thermos. He knelt and picked it up, and when he did, he heard something rattling around inside the hidden compartment. Slowly he unscrewed the bottom and then turned the thermos upside down. Two thumb drives fell out into his hand, the thumb drives he had taken from Anton in Philadelphia. He remembered what Anton had said right before the Romano gunmen entered the room and killed the accountant.

"Did he really hand me thumb drives with access to money on them? The Russians' money?" Chance asked himself.

When Rebecca got to the RV's door, she positioned herself to the side, looked back at Ax, and motioned for him to move up to the other side. Ax stood and slowly moved forward, keeping the AR pointed at the RV. He knew Rebecca would try to kill him right after they killed the man inside.

Chance needed to know what was on the thumb drives, and he needed to know soon. He slowly stood and placed them into his pocket. He then looked out the window above the sink and saw a man moving toward the RV. Chance quickly dropped to a knee and pointed his .45 at the door. He didn't know how many gunmen were outside, but the inside of the RV was no place for him to make a stand against an opposing force. Bullets would make Swiss cheese out of the RV. There was only one thing for him to do. He kept low to the floor and made his way to the bedroom.

When he got there, he lifted the bed and moved it to the side. He then opened the trapdoor under it and dropped out of the RV. He crawled toward the front, took up a position at the corner, and waited. He needed to know how many guns he was up against before he exposed himself.

Rebecca motioned for Ax to go in when she opened the door.

Ax had other plans and shook his head no to his boss.

Rebecca took a deep breath. She was angry, but with nothing left to do, she signaled for him to open the door so she could enter first. Ax agreed and then reached up and grabbed the doorknob.

Chance looked around the factory building, thinking about what to do. Suddenly, he saw his mirror he had hung near his workout equipment. The mirror provided him a view of the front of the RV and the two armed people standing in front of it.

Rebecca nodded her head, and Ax pulled the door open.

Chance took the opportunity and stepped out from the front of the RV.

Ax saw the man come out into the open. He released the door, raised his AR-15 toward the man, and fired carelessly. The bullets struck the side of the RV and the wall behind Chance.

Chance was ready and moved to his left. He fired two shots into the man and directed his attention to the woman. She had fallen when the RV door slammed into her as she was going inside. Rebecca had dropped her gun and moved toward it right before Chance kicked it under the RV.

"That's not a good idea," Chance warned. He grabbed her by the hair, pulled her head back, and placed the barrel under her chin.

"Wait! Wait!" Rebecca pleaded.

"Who sent you?"

"No one sent me. I wanted to collect on the bounty myself," Rebecca confessed. She was scared. She didn't know what he was going to do.

"Who told you how to find me?"

"No one. I just followed you from Freddy's place."

"Who told you I was there?"

"Um, no one. I just—"

Chance slammed her head into the side of the door frame. "I won't ask you again," Chance warned and pulled her head back, preparing to do it again.

"Don't! It was Freddy's girl, Candi. She called me and let me know. I agreed to give her part of the money," Rebecca confessed.

"Leave Las Vegas and never come back. If I ever see you again, I'll kill you." Chance released his grip on her. He then turned and started to walk out of the building. He needed to get to Freddy.

Rebecca held her head as blood trickled down her face. She looked at the AR-15 next to the very-dead Ax, and a thought ran through her mind.

Chance was near the garage door when he heard Rebecca behind him. He knew what she was doing. He quickly turned and saw her lifting the gun. Chance fired two rounds into the woman's chest.

Rebecca Hicks dropped the gun, looked at the man standing in the distance, and slid down the RV steps onto the concrete pad.

CHAPTER 15
IVAN GORKY

Chance left his place in a hurry. He needed information, he needed it quickly, and only one person could get it. On his drive to Freddy's place, Chance called Police Sergeant Parker Denton and told him about the shooting at his place. Parker demanded that Chance go back to the RV to explain why there were three dead people there. Chance refused. He knew he couldn't waste any time sitting in an interrogation room at Metro, explaining why he killed the three contract killers. Morgan needed him more, and that was all that mattered.

The Ford's powerful V-8 roared as Chance sped down the interstate. He needed Freddy, the computer-savvy entrepreneur, to help him in examining the thumb drives. He also wanted to tell the man that his girlfriend, Candi, was leaking information. A leak could get the man who ran the Underground killed.

The interstate was moving slowly, with traffic stacked bumper to bumper at the exits for the Strip. Chance was getting more and more anxious when suddenly his cell phone rang. He picked it up, looked at the caller ID, took a deep breath, and answered the call.

"Well, I know it's Morgan's phone, but I don't think it's her voice I'm about to hear," Chance reluctantly admitted.

"You are correct. I have her, and I'm willing to trade her for the thumb drive that I suspect you have," Leontii stated. The Russian Mafia boss stared at the terrified Morgan sitting on his couch. He had brought her back to his upscale home in the private Desert Oasis Community. "Here, I'll let you say hello." Leontii took his phone from his ear, placed it on speaker, and moved it close to Morgan.

"Chance," Morgan said with a shaken voice.

"Are you okay? Has anyone hurt you?" Chance asked. He was worried about her safety. He knew what the Russians were capable of doing to her.

"Yes, but these Russians need someone to teach them some manners. Maybe you should do it."

"Yeah, is that right?" Chance felt better, knowing Morgan was alive and in good spirits considering her circumstances.

"I want you to do to them what you did to Tony Morreti," Morgan replied, placing emphasis on Tony Morreti's name.

"I will. Where are they holding you?" Chance asked, already knowing where she was. Chance caught on to the clue Morgan provided about Tony Moretti.

"I'm—"

Leontii took the phone away while Igor placed his hand over her mouth.

"Morgan!" Chance yelled into the phone.

"Come now, that's enough talk."

"What about the Muñoz Cartel? You already sold her out to them," Chance said, reminding him about the video he had sold earlier through the Underground.

"They do not have her name, only her face on video. I'll tell them I can't find the woman. Besides, that's not my problem. It's yours and hers. Now, I'll still give Morgan to you, for the thumb drive, but you'll have to deal with Colombians on your own."

"That's bullshit, and you know it!" Chance objected between clenched teeth.

"Call it what you like, but that's the deal. You'll have her alive, and keeping her that way will be up to you. I'll call you later and let you know how we will make the exchange," Leontii stated and quickly ended the call.

Chance was angry. He dropped the phone in the center of the seat and beat his hand against the steering wheel.

Hector Muñoz sat in front of his cold, half-eaten dinner. He was, however, able to finish three glasses of wine. The hours had gone by, and still, there was no phone call from the Russians. He was thinking he had been double-crossed, and when Mariana walked into the room, he could tell by the look on her face there was reason to have doubts.

"What is it?" the patriarch of the Muñoz family asked.

"The Russians called, and they don't have the girl, and they don't think they can get her," Mariana explained and poured herself a glass of wine.

"And what about the money we already paid for her?"

"They said they would refund half the money. The Russians believe they are entitled to the other half since they did give us the video."

"So, they are to decide who gets what. I don't think so. Find me someone who they will trade for, Mariana. It's time to motivate the Russians."

"Yes, Papá." Mariana finished her drink and walked back out of the room. She was tired of the entire ordeal surrounding her brother. It was time to get back to the business that made the Muñoz family the powerful and wealthy cartel they were known for. She believed that her brother's death needed to be avenged but differently.

Edward Romano hung up his phone, lit a cigar, and smiled. He was pleased with what he was able to negotiate with Ivan Gorky. It had taken a few hours, but he was finally able to speak to the Russian Mafia czar. Mr. Romano demanded that Ivan personally deliver the man responsible for his son's death, as per his earlier agreement with Leontii. The Philly Mafia boss had decided he would not work through Leontii, the Gorky's middleman, any longer. During their long telephone call, the two bosses were also able to agree on future mutually profitable business endeavors.

"I guess it's done," Rico asked. He had been sitting nearby and listening to his uncle on the phone for over an hour.

"It is. Soon we'll be leaving Las Vegas. Now, find me some female companionship. I want to celebrate."

"Yes, Uncle."

As the pakhan, or godfather, of the Gorky family, Ivan was not accustomed to having to clean up messes, especially when they were made by Leontii, his most trusted brigadier. After Ivan finished his phone call with Edward Romano, he ordered his bodyguard Michail to ready his jet. It was time for him to leave Moscow for the hot desert sands of Las Vegas. Ivan wasn't looking forward to meeting with the Philly boss. Still, the opportunity of expanding his own organization further into Philadelphia was too great to pass up. First, he needed to speak to his brigadier in Las Vegas and the surrounding lieutenants.

"Michail!" Ivan yelled.

"Yes, Pakhan," Michail answered after running back into the room. Michail was Ivan's top bodyguard. He was once part of an elite military unit. Now, the young man was another kind of soldier, serving under a different flag.

"Make sure Boris and the others are in Las Vegas. I want to speak to all of them. We may be making some changes."

"How many men should I tell to get ready for the trip?" Michail asked. Making changes could mean anything from reorganization to replacing key leaders. In the Russian Mafia, it was nothing like the white-collar corporate world of business. In the Bratva, you were either demoted or simply forced into early retirement. Early retirement didn't come with a severance package, a gold watch, or a nice thank-you for your service to the company.

"Ten should do it."

"Yes, Pakhan," Michail replied and hurried out of the room.

Chance parked in front of Freddy's house and hurried to the door. He made a fist and pounded hard, and he continued to do so until Freddy finally opened it. He didn't allow Freddy to invite him inside. Chance just stepped in and pushed the door open farther, almost knocking the large man over when he saw Candi standing in the living room.

"You! You told them where I was!" Chance yelled as he moved toward the petite woman.

"Chance, stop!" Freddy ordered, but it was of no use. The large man's visitor was angry. He appeared to be all business, and his business was with Candi.

"You told them where I was. Why?" Chance asked as he continued toward the woman, who quickly cowered back until she fell onto the couch.

"Please stop!" Candi pleaded and looked at Freddy for help.

Freddy didn't say anything at first, nor did he move toward them. He had heard what Chance said, and he needed to know what she had possibly done. "Did you tell someone how to find Chance?" Freddy finally asked.

"Freddy, I... Well... It was a lot of money."

Freddy stood still, not saying anything for a moment. For

Freddy, betrayal was the worst sin of them all. He had let Candi into his home, his private business, and of course, his heart. "Leave," Freddy said sternly.

"I need your help and—"

"I wasn't speaking to you, Chance."

"No, Freddy. Please," Candi begged as she stood and slowly moved toward the door.

"I'll give you twenty-four hours, and that's all," Freddy warned as he followed her to the door.

Chance didn't say anything. He just watched the two of them. When Candi got to the door, she stepped out onto the porch and looked at Freddy somberly, hoping he would change his mind.

Freddy took one last look at the woman, and before he shut the door, he repeated himself. "Twenty-four hours, and that's all." Freddy didn't say anything for a few minutes; he just stood at the closed front door. Chance waited until the man was ready to talk.

"What happened?" Freddy asked as he headed for the dining room and his computer that sat on the table.

"She had Rebecca Hicks and two other men come at me," Chance explained as he followed the big man.

"And…"

"And, I had to put them down hard."

"What do you need?" Freddy asked.

"I need to know where everyone in the Gorky family and the Muñoz Cartel is right now," Chance answered.

"What about the Romano family?" Freddy asked as he typed away on his computer.

"I don't know anything about the Romano family. Why do you ask?" Chance questioned with a blank look on his face. He remembered what Parker had said in the hospital, but he didn't know the Romanos were in play now.

Freddy turned around. "They're here for you," he

proclaimed to a shocked Chance Hardway. "Apparently, the Russians told Edward Romano that you killed his son, Junior. The Russians are supposed to have already delivered you to them. I think they used Morgan and her problem with the Muñoz Cartel to draw you out into the open." Freddy offered Chance a chair.

Chance took a seat and let out a deep breath. "Their plan is working. They have Morgan."

"Do you know where?" Freddy asked.

"Yes, they're somewhere in the Desert Oasis."

"Give me a minute," the computer whiz stated as he typed away on his keypad. "I got it!"

"What?"

"The Gorky family owns a house there. It's at 11416 Desert Rose Avenue. They have it listed under the Mount Elbrus Trust."

"Mount Elbrus?" Chance asked.

"Yeah, it's the highest peak in Europe. It sits within the Caucasus Mountains. It's an old dormant volcano."

"Really?" Chance asked, surprised by the useless information the man had swirling around in his head.

"Yeah. You plan on going to get her?"

"Freddy, can I trust you—I mean really trust you?" Chance asked.

"I think we have to trust each other. I don't know how but someone in the Gorky organization may know I'm involved. They used the Underground to get to you. I mean, somehow you knew I was the Underground, and then there's Candi. I also think that if you're dead, then I'll be killed for helping you locate their men. I know you didn't kill all of them, but that won't matter to the Russians. So, all we got right now is each other."

"Who do you think's pulling the strings?" Chance asked. He had to trust someone, and he figured it might as well be the man who seemed to know everything.

"I've been working on that ever since I told you I thought someone was making a move on the Gorky family," Freddy explained. He then spun the computer monitor so Chance could view it. "Here we have—"

"Impressive," Chance whispered as he moved closer to view the detailed Gorky organization command structure. Freddy had photos of everyone associated with the Russian crime family and their known addresses, affiliates, and anything else he felt was essential to know about each individual.

"Thanks. Here we have Ivan Gorky at the top. He's the godfather, or pakhan, and he's in charge of everything. If he orders something, it's done, no questions asked. Now, here—"

"I know Leontii Adamovich," Chance stated.

"Yeah, well, he's a brigadier, or the second in command. He runs things here in Las Vegas mainly, but he also oversees Chicago, Los Angeles, and Philly. He has people in those cities who report to him. See, all these guys here are lieutenants. Well, not these two anymore. They're dead," Freddy explained and pointed at the pictures of Vasily Zlobin and Vladimir Dudko. "So is he, but you knew that."

"Yeah, I did," Chance stated after Freddy pointed at Victor's image, the man who had cut Morgan and the man he killed. "What about Anton here?" Chance asked.

"He's the bookkeeper or accountant. Up until he died, Anton kept a close eye on Philly as well. That's where the Bratva are trying to expand to if they can work something out with the Italians. Anton's main job was keeping track of the family's money."

"All their money?"

"Yeah, the Russians don't trust very many people. You must understand, this guy had everything he could ask for. He was given money, women, and anything else he desired. They kept this guy happy so he wouldn't take their money and run."

"I need you to do something," Chance said and pulled the two thumb drives from his pocket.

"What's this?"

"I hope it's money."

"Money?" Freddy asked excitedly and inserted them into his computer. After a few moments, he turned and looked at Chance with a surprised expression.

"What is it?" Chance asked.

"Money. A lot of money."

Hector Muñoz and his two men returned to the house around two o'clock in the morning. When he walked inside the foyer, he was met by Mariana. She had some news and needed to share it with the head of the Muñoz Cartel.

"What is it, Mariana?"

"Our people have been working all night trying to get something. I didn't think we would get anything, but then about an hour ago, one of our people learned Ivan Gorky is flying into Las Vegas later this morning. He'll arrive at around ten o'clock."

"Very well, this is what I was looking for. Get him and bring him to me," Hector ordered and walked by Mariana toward the living room.

"That could be extremely dangerous. It could start a war with the Russians," the Witch Captain of Colombia warned as she followed behind the patriarch.

Hector stopped and turned abruptly to face his daughter. He was angry and did not want to be questioned. "I'm not afraid of war, and neither should you be. We are the Muñoz Cartel! We are descendants of great fighters whose origins go all the way back to Bogotá when we fought for our independence from the Spanish."

"Yes, Papá," Mariana said and started to walk away.

"I'm still the leader, and you will obey my commands. I will not be questioned by a woman. You know nothing of men and war!"

Mariana was upset but did not show it. Her father's words hurt; they drove through her like a dagger. There were brief occasions when he complimented her on the successes she had made for the cartel, yet there were other occasions when his true colors made an appearance. Hector Muñoz was, like other men in the cartel, a misogynist.

When she entered the office to make the necessary arrangements, she found Manuel, sitting in the leather chair behind the desk. Manuel was a handsome man from Southern Colombia. He had been in the cartel for many years and was considered Hector's best lieutenant. Mariana believed Manuel wanted to be more than a lieutenant within the cartel, and if she didn't keep a close eye on him, then maybe he would be.

"How is Hector?" Manuel asked.

"He's fine. Please get up so I can make some arrangements," Mariana ordered as she walked around the desk and stood over Manuel.

"Sí, señora." Manuel stood and removed himself from behind the desk. "Is there anything you need from me?" he asked after moving to the other side of the desk, to the subordinate spot where soldiers stood to receive orders.

"There's a plane coming in at ten o'clock. There's someone on it who we're going to grab and bring back to my father." Mariana sat back in the chair and crossed her legs.

"Who is this person?"

"Ivan Gorky."

"That will be very dangerous," Manuel warned. He knew Ivan Gorky was the Russian Mafia leader, and kidnapping him would undoubtedly have long-lasting consequences.

"I know, but it's what my father ordered."

"What do you think about this order, Mariana?"

"I, like you, am not to question the orders of my father. Now go and make the necessary arrangements. I'm putting the success or the failure of this job on you," Mariana declared before answering her cell phone. She looked at Manuel sternly before saying anything to the caller on the phone.

"Sí, señora," Manuel replied and made his way out of the office. He was angry, so he hurried out of the house through the front door and slammed it on the way out. When he was finally outside and away from anyone else, he released a tirade of profanity directed at la Capitana Bruja de Colombia. Manuel, unlike the other men, didn't believe Mariana was a witch. He also thought it was only a matter of time before the once-powerful Muñoz Cartel fell, providing an opportunity for a man like himself to take over. "No woman has the strength to run a cartel," Manuel declared. He then made the necessary arrangements to abduct Ivan Gorky, which was an act that could lead to the fall of the Muñoz Cartel and the rise of Manuel Louis Vargas. Manuel relished the thought.

CHAPTER 16
THE LONGSHOT

Boris paced back and forth in his suite's living room with his phone to his ear as he listened intently to Leontii explain what he planned on doing with Morgan and Chance Hardway. He was surprised to learn Ivan was on his way to Las Vegas, which was not particularly good for Leontii. Boris believed his plan was starting to come together.

When Leontii ended the phone call, Boris walked to the window. He watched the tourists sunning themselves around the pool below. While he stood there, he thought through things.

If Ivan has determined he must come to Las Vegas to take care of a situation that Leontii failed to do, then it's because he's doubting his brigadier's ability to run the business. Therefore, he must be looking to replace him very soon, Boris thought to himself.

"Good news, comrade?" Pavel asked from the couch. He and Maxim, who was sitting in the chair next to him, had followed Boris's orders and kept out of sight since arriving in Las Vegas. Both were eager to start moving forward in some direction. They felt any direction was better than sitting around and waiting.

"Yes, Ivan is coming."

Maxim sat forward with a concerned look on his face. "When?"

"It's okay, my friend. It means he has doubts about Leontii as a leader," Boris explained. "You need a drink." The lieutenant walked over and poured two glasses of bourbon. He then calmly walked over and handed them to his men.

"What's your plan?" Pavel asked after taking a drink. The assassin had brought some of the tools of his trade with him. He needed to know if they would be required.

"I need to think. We must be cautious about moving forward. One mistake could cost us our lives. Don't worry, Pavel, I'll let you know if we need your special skills."

Chance made phone calls to a few people he trusted, to make arrangements and to get additional information. He then sat on the couch and anxiously waited for Freddy as he worked through the thumb drives' different files. While Freddy kept busy, Chance looked at the printout of the Gorkys' organization structure. He needed to know who was attempting to make a move on Ivan Gorky. As he glared at the paper, he heard Freddy typing feverishly at the keyboard.

Chance noticed there were five men highlighted on the paper as deceased. The dead men were Anton, Vladimir, Vasily, Igor, Sava, and Luca. Freddy's chart appeared to be mostly accurate. Chance closed his eyes, leaned back against the couch, and thought about the five men. *All of them had a hand in hurting Morgan.* Chance thought.

Chance opened his eyes and spoke, "All but one!"

"What?" a startled Freddy asked.

"Where's Boris?" Chance asked after running toward Freddy.

Freddy turned back to face his computer and maneuvered

through the countless emails he had saved. He moved to the ones he had not opened in the Underground's email account. After a few minutes, he turned back toward Chance with a smile. "Boris Yelchin is here."

"How do you know? Do people just email you information without anyone asking for it?" Chance asked.

"Yes, actually. I get emails and text messages with very vague information in them, like what I received about you when you were going after the Bratva. Now, in this email here, someone simply typed one name in it, Boris Yelchin. So, let's say I knew of someone who was looking for Boris, then I would contact the person who sent this email and offer to purchase information."

"Offer to buy it," Chance instructed.

"You have some money?" Freddy asked with a slight smirk on his face.

"Yeah, here." Chance pulled a stack of hundreds from his back pocket.

"Isn't that the money I gave you earlier?"

"Yeah."

Freddy shook his head. It was apparent the men viewed money differently. "Keep it. I already made an offer. We're just waiting to see if this seller takes it."

"How much did you offer?" Chance asked.

"Three hundred."

"Is it enough?"

"It depends on who it is. If it's a valet, it won't be. If it's a bellhop or room service employee, then it is. If it's anyone else, I don't know," Freddy explained and waited for a response to come back.

While they waited, Chance looked at the chart once more. He saw a man in the organization whose status he didn't think was updated. "This guy's dead." Chance held the paper in front of Freddy and pointed at the image of a man identified as Pavel.

"It's updated. He's not dead," Freddy said and looked back at the screen. "It's a valet. He wants a grand," Freddy stated after reading the response.

Chance looked at the chart once more, surprised by what Freddy had said about the man known as Pavel. Chance recognized his picture. He was the man who had been passed out on the yacht with a woman next to him. *He should have died in the explosion, but he wasn't... because he's the one who blew up the ship, killing Vasily Zlobin and everyone else on board. That's why I was so close to shore. He escaped with me in the raft, knowing I would be blamed for it,* Chance thought to himself. "What about this guy?" Chance asked and pointed at a man with the name Maxim under his image.

"He's alive too," Freddy answered after glancing at the man in the picture. He was getting ready to send the confirmation agreeing to the price when Chance reached down and grabbed his arm.

"Wait, send the images of these two men to the seller and ask if he knows where they are," Chance instructed, and Freddy sent it off to the unknown seller. It didn't take long before they received a response.

"Great! Now he wants five grand," Freddy said, disappointed.

"Pay it."

"All right. Aces and eights," Freddy mumbled. The man knew he was in too deep with Chance to back out now. He had to keep betting on the man he believed was holding nothing but the fatal dead man's hand. "I hope you got an ace in the hole. All of this is about to get really crazy, and you're going to need all the help you can get."

Chance's eyes widened. "It's a longshot but it's all I got, and I'm all in. No aces."

Freddy thought for a second. "I might have a wild card. I'll make some calls. Sometimes the longshots payout the best."

"Okay, but keep working on the thumb drives and find out where the guys are. I'll be back as quickly as I can."

"Where're you going?" Freddy asked.

"Shopping. I need some supplies. By the way, what do you know about hotel security cameras and hacking?"

"Some." Freddy answered with a smile on his face.

The house was decorated in an Italian villa theme. The foyer was circular in light brown and white, with white columns supporting the second-floor walkway. There were two sets of stairs, one on each side of the foyer. The living room was large, with a high ceiling that had exposed wood trusses extending across. The interior was painted in a dark brown with splashes of light brown, providing an old look. If Morgan were not being held hostage, she probably would have felt comfortable in the elaborate mansion.

"Will you accompany me for a late dinner?" Leontii asked as he walked past her. He had already untied her and allowed her to move about somewhat freely if she had one of Leontii's men with her.

Morgan sat in a leather chair and crossed her arms. "I'm not hungry."

"Then you can watch me eat," the brigadier stated and snapped his fingers at his man, Sacha, who was standing next to Morgan. Sacha grabbed Morgan by the arm and dragged her into the dining room, where Leontii took a seat at the head of the dining table. "I'm having a delicious meal. It's a Russian dish consisting of lamb, beef, and pork wrapped in a flour dough. It has garlic, peppers, and onions mixed in. It's delicious. Are you sure you're not hungry?" Leontii asked and took a bite.

Morgan was forced to sit next to Leontii while Igor sat directly across from her, enjoying his dinner. "I said I wasn't hungry. Besides, I don't want anything from you."

"Not hungry, interesting. I'm hungry, Igor's hungry, and Sacha is also hungry. Maybe not for food, but hungry. We all are. In America, people have much of everything, but in Russia, it's not so. Hunger is not something that can be taught. It must be experienced. The Bratva is full of men who desired more than what they had. They're men who were beaten, starved, frozen, and discarded by others as children. They became who they are by the hunger that drove them to survive and want more out of life. It is why we prosper here in your country."

"No, you steal, hurt, and kill whomever, as long as it benefits you. You and the others are nothing. You're not even a real man," Morgan declared. Once again, she leaned back in her chair and crossed her arms, then watched coolly as Igor stood with his eyes bulging and fists clenched.

"I'll beat you—"

"No, Igor!" Leontii grabbed the man's arm and guided him back into his chair. "Please eat your dinner. We cannot harm her, yet." Leontii knew Morgan was too valuable of a hostage whom he needed to keep safe and sound until he got what he needed. "You did not flinch when Igor stood up so abruptly, are you not afraid?"

"I'm only afraid of one thing," Morgan stated.

"What would that be?"

"I'm afraid Chance will die trying to save me."

"So, she's worried you and I will kill her boyfriend," Igor stated and laughed aloud with a mouthful of the Russian food.

"No, Igor. I'm not worried you'll kill him. I know Chance will, without a doubt, kill all three of you in this room. I'm just afraid it won't end there. He'll continue to kill each and every one of you who comes for me, even if it will eventually cost him his life."

"Chance Hardway will not kill me!" Igor declared.

Morgan leaned forward and looked at Igor smugly. "I bet

174

that's exactly what your woman-beating, cowardly brother thought too, right before he took his last breath."

"You fucking whore!" Igor yelled. He dove over the table and grabbed Morgan by the shirt.

Morgan stood and grabbed the wine bottle sitting on the table. Leontii jumped from his chair and tried to restrain his man.

"Stop, Igor!" Leontii yelled as Morgan tried to pull away.

Sacha had his arms around Morgan with his hands on Igor's wrist, trying to free the woman. It took a moment, but Igor finally let go.

He looked up at Morgan from the table. "Whore!" he roared.

Morgan swung the wine bottle at his head. The glass shattered upon impact and knocked the man out. She grabbed the knife next to Leontii's plate and quickly swung it at his face, cutting him deeply across the cheek.

Sacha forced the knife from Morgan's hand. Leontii used his napkin and covered the bloody wound. He hurried to the mirror on the wall next to the China cabinet to examine the cut. Anger and rage filled his eyes when he saw the gash. He turned and faced his assailant, and without thinking, he went at the woman. He punched her repeatedly while Sacha, reluctantly, held her up. When Morgan went unconscious, Sacha released her and let her slip to the floor, but that didn't stop Leontii. He continued to kick her in the ribs.

"Brigadier, you need her!" Sacha shouted, hoping it would stop his boss.

Leontii stopped and peered at his man. "Take her to the bedroom," Leontii ordered. He watched as Sacha picked her up and carried her away. The Russian boss then walked back to his chair and sat. He knew he had possibly hurt his chances of getting the thumb drive from Hardway. Leontii shook his head, disgusted with himself for losing his temper.

Slowly, Igor came to. "What happened?" he asked, right before Leontii delivered a right cross to the side of his face, knocking him out once more.

Sacha carried Morgan to a bedroom, opened the curtains, and peered out toward the hills. He then walked to the small bedroom bar. He opened the refrigerator underneath it and took out some ice. He wrapped the ice in a rag and gently placed it on the beaten woman's cheek. He checked out the window once more, then looked at Morgan. He didn't like beating women, nor did he like the way the Bratva treated them. Sacha left the room to allow the woman to sleep. He sat in a chair outside her door and looked through his phone. Sacha spent his time responding to some previous texts from an American friend he had missed earlier. He conversed with them until late into the morning hours, while waiting for more orders from Leontii.

Morgan couldn't tell what time it was, but she knew it was late. Her face, side, and arms hurt. She slowly lifted her hand to her left eye and felt the puffiness of the swelling around it. The beating was terrible but not as bad as the last one. However, she did get some satisfaction knowing she scarred the man who was responsible for scaring her.

Ivan Gorky and his men had been in the air for a few hours when he finally took a seat to relax with a glass of bourbon. The long flight gave the pakhan plenty of time to think about what had been transpiring under Leontii's command. He was questioning Leontii's leadership decisions. Thus far, the brigadier had not recovered the family's money. He had also made a deal with the Romano family and failed to deliver on it. Now, Ivan wondered what other failures Leontii had that he didn't know about. The boss also speculated that the once-trusted brigadier could be making a move on him. Ivan soon came to think there was a possibility he was walking into a trap.

Ivan stepped into the main cabin. "Michail, come back here."

Michail was sitting up front, along with the other men, when his pakhan called for him. The trusted bodyguard jumped to his feet and rushed to the back of the plane.

"Yes, Pakhan."

"Shut the door," Ivan said softly.

Michail did as he was told and turned back toward his employer.

Ivan looked him over and offered him a seat in one of the other chairs. "Michail, I trust you more than any other. I've come to realize that we may be walking into a trap in Las Vegas."

"I will tell the pilot immediately, and we will land somewhere else," Michail quickly stated and stood.

"No, we will still land in Las Vegas, but I want you and the others to be ready for anything."

"We will," Michail stated and started to walk out of the plane's private suite.

"Michail, one more thing."

"Yes."

Ivan walked over and placed his right hand on Michail's shoulder. "I have the ransom money in the account just in case I'm taken hostage and they demand a ransom. If I'm killed, use the money to avenge my murder. Whatever money is left is to be yours." He paused for a moment while looking into his most trusted man's eyes. "And if something does happen to me, you must kill all responsible, even if it's our own people. No one is beyond your reach or fury. I mean no one," Ivan stated, clarifying that Michail answered to no one in the pakhan's absence or death.

"I will do whatever is needed, to anyone," Michail said, confirming he understood what was to be done.

Chance met Earl at his place in the desert. Earl was one of the few people Chance trusted. The two had spent time in various combat zones around the world. They had experienced things that changed them forever. For Earl, it changed him a lot more than Chance. The once-fit operator was now overweight, a smoker, and probably drank more than he should. Earl had helped Chance with the Golden Ring, and now Chance needed him again.

"I'll be there," Earl assured after putting a duffle bag into the bed of Chance's truck. He pulled a flask from his pocket and took a long drink.

"I need to be able to count on you," Chance stated as he made his way back toward the driver's door.

"You can. I'll be ready."

"What about the other thing I asked you to do?" Chance asked.

"It's done. We got eyes on the target and a sleeper in place."

"Can we trust them?"

"As much as you can trust me. By the way, that was my last drink until we're done. I've never let you down, and I won't now," Earl declared to Chance before walking back toward his barn.

Chance watched the man stagger as he carried his heavy frame across the sandy ground. He knew Earl fought the demons in his head regularly. As Chance drove away, he wondered if he was adding more demons to the fight.

Freddy was still working at his computer when Chance came back inside, carrying a duffle bag. Chance placed the bag down and took his seat next to Freddy once more. He leaned forward and looked at the screen.

"Did you find anything?"

"Yeah, Boris has got to be the one making a move on the Gorky family. See, these accounts are from Anton's thumb drives, and they are being funneled into these accounts. I ran a hack on one of the banks the money is being funneled into and discovered Boris Yelchin is the account holder," Freddy explained.

"Anything else?"

"Yeah, a lot. Anton was skimming a lot of money, and it's all on this other thumb drive. Boris has a hacker in California breaking into the accounts, but he's pretty slow at it. I've already stopped him, and I'm putting the money into other accounts I've created."

"Good. I need you to create a bank account under this name and put five million from the money Anton already skimmed into it," Chance instructed and handed Freddy a piece of paper with a name on it. He then went to his duffle bag and started taking his tools out.

"Who's this?" Freddy asked.

"A friend. Just do it."

"What about the rest of the money?"

"Put three million of Ivan's money into three separate accounts. Put the access to those accounts on separate thumb drives. Then divide the rest of his money equally into two accounts. Finally, keep some for yourself."

"How much am I to keep for myself?" Freddy asked.

"Enough that won't draw any attention and enough that no one will come looking for you to get it back. Did you find out where Boris and the other two are?" Chance asked as he pulled the bulletproof vest out of the duffle.

"Yeah, all three are staying at the Winecup Hotel and Casino," Freddy replied.

Chance knew of the hotel and casino located off the strip. "Anything else?" he asked as he prepared his gear.

"Yeah, I was looking through my other emails while my hacking software worked on the thumb drives, and it looks like a lot of people are in town."

"Who?"

"Ivan Gorky is flying in on his private jet. Hector Muñoz and his people are here, and of course, Edward Romano is here, but you already knew that."

"Okay, I got a lot of work to do," Chance stated and then checked the action on his compact 9 mm.

"What are you going to do?" Freddy asked, concerned.

"Level the playing field."

CHAPTER 17
EARLY MORNING VISITOR

Leontii was lying on the couch in the living room, trying not to move as the doctor closed the cut on his face. Doctor Walter Newton was a renowned surgeon with a gambling problem. Because of that gambling problem, he had a large debt that had him working for the Russians. Doctor Newton used lidocaine to numb the area around the wound. Still, the cut was deep, and the numbing solution only took the edge off.

Igor sat on the other side of the room in a leather chair, watching the doctor work. He didn't say anything. He knew he had made a mistake, a big mistake.

"Well, that's all I can do for you here," the doctor said as he gathered his medical tools.

Leontii disappointedly looked across the room at Igor and then back at the doctor. "How bad is it?" Leontii asked.

"You'll need more work, by a plastic surgeon, if you don't want a scar. Some nerves may have been severed, which could affect your facial expressions. All I can do here is close the wound."

Leontii stood and grabbed the small handheld mirror from the coffee table. He held it up to his face and examined the large cut. He then looked at Igor once more.

Igor looked down at the ground, unable to face his brigadier.

"I'll set you up with a plastic surgeon for tomorrow," Doctor Newton stated and then stood and started for the door.

"Wait! There's another patient you must treat," Leontii snapped as he walked to the dining room table.

"The whore doesn't need any doctor! She's lucky to be alive!" Igor blurted and then looked away from his boss once more. He couldn't look him in the eye knowing he was the reason the man had suffered.

"It's not for the whore. Take off your shirt," Leontii ordered while holding the knife Morgan had used to cut him.

"Yes, Brigadier," Igor said as he removed his shirt and dropped to his knees. The big Russian knew what was coming. He closed his eyes, tilted his head forward, and took a deep breath as Brigadier Leontii walked toward him.

"Look, I'm not here wanting to be a witness or anything like that," Doctor Newton stated.

"Shut up and sit down!" Leontii loudly ordered as he pointed the knife toward the shaking and frightened medical professional.

"Okay. I'll sit here," the doctor stated and sat in an uncomfortable armchair near the front door.

Leontii slowly made his way behind his number-one man and took a hard stance. He ran his left hand over Igor's shoulder softly, pushed Igor's head to the left, and held it there.

Igor knew what was coming. He also knew he deserved it.

Leontii bent down and whispered into Igor's ear, "You must learn to control yourself. Do not scream," the Brigadier ordered.

Igor braced himself.

Leontii looked at the large threatening shepherd tattoo on Igor's shoulder. It was a mark of honor. He had been given the tattoo after being promoted to a protector. The brigadier placed the knife's edge against Igor's skin and began cutting the man's tattoo off.

Igor did as he was ordered. He did not scream, nor did he move. He just looked down and breathed deeply.

After Edward Romano's conversation with Ivan Gorky, he became paranoid and was concerned about his safety. He decided to move from the Galleria Hotel and Casino to a place more suited for himself, his men, and the people running security. The Tease was a renovated hotel and casino near Fremont Street. In its earlier years, it was run by the Italian mob, and over the years, it had been seized by the federal government more than once. Now, it was supposedly owned by a private company but was rumored to be under mob control once again. Freddy had found where Edward Romano was staying and gave the location to Chance before he left earlier.

Chance borrowed Freddy's car and parked it behind his bar, away from the melee of Fremont Street. He entered through the back door of Freddy's and made his way to the front where he had a view of the Tease. It was three o'clock in the morning, but Fremont Street was still crowded with late-hour partiers. They danced and drank while they stumbled back to their hotel rooms. The Tease was ten stories high with a casino on the main floor. Two large entrances opened to Fremont, where hotel security stood guard. Chance had been in the casino a few times, and he recalled that the kitchen was on the right side of the casino floor, and it could be accessed from the alley. He also knew the hotel had security personnel walking the casino floor and the halls. They would also have people inside the security office, scanning the overhead cameras that Freddy should have already hacked into. He had to get by them without being noticed. He took out his cell phone and dialed the big man's number.

"I'm in." Freddy said happily after answering the call.

"Good, what do you see?"

"Hotel security and men who look like they work for the Romano family all over the place."

"I thought so. I'm going in through the kitchen."

"Okay, all the cameras are on a loop from the previous four hours. You should be good for a while." Freddy advised.

Chance walked out of Freddy's, locked the front door behind him, and casually walked across Fremont, politely dodging the partiers as he did so. When he reached the alley, he maneuvered past a delivery truck, grabbed a box of tomatoes off the back of it, and walked inside the hotel. Chance was relieved to find there weren't many of the kitchen staff inside. He laid the tomatoes on a counter and quickly made his way toward the casino floor.

At the door, he paused and peered out onto the floor and saw more hotel security, cocktail waitresses, and other people who worked inside the Tease. He also saw a few men who he believed were not in Las Vegas on vacation. The men wore suits and expensive shoes and appeared to be Italian. *Edward Romano brought an army,* Chance thought as he looked for something to help him get around the hotel without being seen. He was trying to think through his options when the door opened, surprising him.

"I'm sorry, but you can't be back here," the security guard said after nearly bumping into the man. He believed the man was just another intoxicated and confused guest of the Tease.

"I'm sorry. I'm just a little lost," Chance said while slurring his words as he placed his hands on the man's arms.

"That's okay. What room are you in?" the man asked as he lifted the drunken man up.

"I forgot. I'm here with the Romano party."

"Oh, you're one of his men. Okay, c'mon, you guys got both the ninth and tenth floors, but you look like one of his guys on the ninth."

Chance stopped his drunken act, looked at the man, and smiled. "Thanks for the information."

"Wait! Who are you?" the security guard asked as he reached for his walkie-talkie. It was no use. Chance gripped the man's suit coat to pull him into him and then delivered a headbutt to the bewildered man's head, knocking him out. Chance caught the man from falling, looked around to make sure no one saw, and dragged the unconscious man into the supply closet to the right of him.

It was late, and the bedroom was dark and cold. Morgan couldn't sleep. She lay there quietly on the king-size bed for hours, running countless scenarios through her mind, all of which focused on trying to find a way out of the situation she and Chance were in. "Damn it!" she whispered and slammed her hand onto the bed. No matter how Morgan played it out in her mind, she couldn't find a safe way out for them. The Muñoz Cartel would not rest until she was dead. The Russians would kill her for what Chance had done to their men.

Morgan closed her eyes, and tears rolled down her cheeks. She allowed herself to escape once more to the fictional world where her children ran freely on the beach while Chance sat next to her under the sun in a tropical oasis somewhere. The fantasy provided a sense of warmth and safety. Before long, she drifted off to sleep with Chance's voice whispering in her ear, "I love you."

Downstairs, Doctor Newton applied a dressing to Igor's wound. There was nothing for the man with a medical degree to do except cover the cut with a sterile dressing. Leontii wasn't allowing the good doctor to reattach the skin he had removed from the man who had failed him. As the doctor finished his work, Leontii handed Igor a glass of whiskey.

"I'll never fail you again."

"I know, and scars heal. You can earn back what you have lost," Leontii stated and held his glass up for a toast. "To the Bratva."

"To the Bratva," Igor repeated.

Doctor Newton once again gathered his medical tools and put them in his bag. He desperately wanted to leave. When he got to the door, he grabbed the knob, opened it, and took a step.

"Doctor, please keep your phone nearby. I may need you again later," Leontii said and finished his brandy.

"I don't know if I'll be around, I—"

"You better be. I wouldn't want to call on your pretty little wife just to have her help me find you."

"No, no, that won't be necessary. I'll be around."

"Good, I thought you might."

Chance stepped out of the supply closet wearing a new suit of clothes. The coat was a little oversized in the shoulders, and the pants were loose around his waist, but he figured no one would really notice. People tended not to see the security personnel in the casinos; they were a reminder to the tourists that some laws and rules had to be followed, even in Sin City.

After leaving the kitchen, Chance confidently walked across the casino floor to the elevators. A room service cart sat inside the elevator with a half-eaten hamburger on it. Chance used the keycard he had found in the security guard's coat pocket and slid it into the slot, giving him access to the tenth floor. Soon the doors closed, and he was on his way up.

He grew anxious as each floor passed. After the fifth floor, Chance reached around to the middle of his back to ready his gun. Then the elevator stopped on the sixth floor, and the doors opened. Chance placed his hands back in front of his body and waited nervously.

Rocky, Brando, and Marcello got on the elevator when the doors opened. The three men were on their way up to relieve the others standing guard on the tenth floor. The Romano men were working two-hour shifts around the clock protecting their boss, Edward Romano. They had just finished a sweep of the fifth floor when they crossed paths with the security guard.

"Where are you on your way to, Mr. Liston?" Rocky asked after tilting his head to read the name tag on Chance's coat.

Chance looked at the man and then at the others. He sized each of them up quickly. "The tenth floor. I've got to make my rounds."

Marcello looked at the security guard suspiciously as the doors closed. He placed his hands on his hips. "Oddly, no one from security has come up to the tenth floor since we got here."

"That is odd," Chance agreed and then reached over and pushed the emergency stop button, halting the elevator between floors.

"What are you doing? Why are we stopping?" Brando asked. He was farsighted and wasn't wearing his glasses. He leaned closer to the elevator panel and squinted at the words on the button. "Emergency stop. Why did you press that?"

Rocky and Marcello looked at each other, and suddenly their eyes lit up. Chance didn't allow the men to strike first. He punched Rocky in the throat, dropping him to his knees quickly. He then delivered two quick jabs to Marcello, one strike for each of the man's eyes. Marcello stumbled back; he was stunned. Brando, who was late to the party, drew his gun, but Chance knocked it out of his hands with a quick kick. He drove the palm of his hand upward under the chin of the would-be gunman, sending him back. Chance used his foot and kept Brando pinned against the wall. At the same time, he delivered elbows into Marcello's face until the man fell to the elevator floor, unconscious.

Rocky regained his ability to breathe and charged at their

attacker. He threw his arms around the man's waist, forged forward, and grabbed the handle along the wall, trapping the security guard. Brando ran over and took advantage of the situation, punching the security guard in the face.

Chance used his hands and arms to block the blows to his head as best as he could. When Brando stopped to look for his dropped gun, Chance took the opportunity to push Rocky off.

Rocky was a bigger man, so now he was out of breath. He staggered and reached for his gun. Chance ran forward and grabbed Rocky by the back of his head, then brought it down hard and fast onto his knee, knocking him out.

Brando finally found his gun under Marcello and pulled it free but found Chance ready for him. Chance grabbed the man's gun hand as he swung it around, then punched him four times above his left eye. The man blinked twice before falling against the wall, where his blood dripped to the floor.

Chance used the unconscious men's neckties and bound the three of them to the elevator's wall handle. He then used the mirrored door to straighten his clothes and to clean his face before turning the elevator back on.

When the elevator reached the tenth floor, Chance prepared himself for another fight. When the doors opened, he was surprised to find there was no guard. He thought for a second and stepped back inside to grab the room service cart. He cleaned it off and tried to make it look neat. He cautiously made his way to the corner of the wall and peered down the hallway, where he found two men standing in front of one suite.

"What's the best play?" Chance whispered to himself, then suddenly, he had an idea. He removed all the dishes from the cart except for two coffee cups and an empty metal coffee pot. *Who drinks coffee with a hamburger?* Chance thought as he threw the half-eaten burger into the trash can next to him.

It was late, and both Dino and Angel were getting tired.

Both men knew somewhere inside the comfortable suite they currently guarded, their boss was sleeping peacefully. All either man wanted to do was to get down to the ninth floor and climb into bed. They had been in Las Vegas for a while now, and neither had had an opportunity to rest. Dino was sitting in a chair that he had taken from another suite and was about to doze off when he heard a service cart coming down the hall.

Angel stepped in front of the cart, stopping Chance a few feet from the door. "Can I help you?" the tall thin man asked.

"Yeah, I ran into some of your men on the sixth floor. They said I should bring some coffee up to you guys." Chance lifted the metal pot as he stepped to the side of the cart, bettering his position.

Dino stood and walked to the cart. "I could use some," he said as he reached for the other cup.

"Good," Chance replied and swung the pot at Dino's head. He caught him perfectly on the left side of his temple. The man fell back, dazed.

"What the—"

The other side of the coffee pot struck the right side of Angel's head. He took the blow harder than his friend Dino. The shorter man dropped to the floor, completely unconscious. Chance quickly came back, grabbed Dino by the shirt, and punched him in the jaw until he, too, lost consciousness.

Chance looked around and prepared himself for reinforcements, but none came. He searched both men until he found the room key to the suite. Quietly, he slid the card reader into the slot in the door and waited until the light turned green, then opened the door and cautiously stepped inside. The place was dark. Chance walked around the suite, checking each room, but found no one else. He saved what he thought was the master suite for last. Before going inside, Chance went back out into the hallway and dragged Angel and Dino inside, where he secured them with lamp cords he had found in the room suite. With both guards tied up, Chance slowly opened the door leading into the master suite.

Edward Romano didn't know how long he had been sleeping, but when he felt someone kicking his mattress, he knew it wasn't time to get up. He opened his eyes, lifted himself up, and turned to face his early morning visitor. Romano didn't know who it was, but he could tell it was a man. Right now, the man was nothing more than a silhouette in the light of the rising sun at his back.

"Who are you, and what do you want?" the notorious crime boss asked.

"I'm the man you're looking for. I'm also the man who will decide if you get to see another sunrise." Chance turned the nightstand light on and moved into the light, allowing Edward Romano Sr. to get a clear look at him.

"So, you're here to kill me?"

"Only if I have to."

Romano reached for his glasses on the nightstand and put them on. He then looked very closely at the man he had come to kill. "What are we to do now?" he asked and crossed his arms after sitting back against the headboard.

"We talk."

CHAPTER 18
MAKING DEALS

Edward Romano Sr. didn't know what Chance Hardway wanted to talk about, but whatever it was, he really wasn't in the mood to listen. Hardway was the man who had killed his son, and that wasn't something he was about to let go. It wasn't something he could live with. It also wasn't something others would allow him to live with either.

"Well, you seem to have my undivided attention," Romano stated as he nodded at the gun in Chance's hand.

Chance looked at his gun and the silencer attached to it. He then looked back up at the Philly crime boss. "I'm not here to kill you."

"Oh, is that something you reserve for people like my son?"

"I didn't kill your son."

"What do you mean? Leontii Adamovich told me you were responsible for his death. You can't lie your way out of this."

"I'm not trying to. I was there, but I didn't kill him. Now, I did kill some of the men who were hired to kill the witness, but that's all. Your son was killed by one of the hired guns when he tried to escape wearing a US Marshals jacket."

"Leontii told me you did it."

Chance laughed. "Well, I'm sure he told you a lot of things, but I would guess most of those are not true as well."

"How do I know I can believe you?"

"You can't. It's all about telling the truth and hoping we believe each other."

"Truths, what other truths are there?" Romano asked.

"Well, I'll tell you I'm the one who came to Philadelphia to get Junior. I'm the one who handed him over to the feds, and I'm the one who killed your men who came at me at Anton's home, and that was self-defense, by the way," Chance explained and waited for a response.

Romano closed his eyes and thought about everything for a moment before speaking. "In our business, yours included, we are all responsible for the lives we take, self-defense or not. You've killed some of my people, which isn't something that can be easily overlooked."

"You know, I find it hard to believe you actually feel as though you are in some position to negotiate," Chance indicated as he stood and pointed the gun at the mobster's head.

"You don't understand the position I'm in, Mr. Hardway. What am I to tell my men if I left without killing you? Reparations have got to be made."

"How about me getting to you without killing any of your men? Right now, five of your men are beaten, but they're alive. How about me walking out of here without leaving your brains splattered on the wall behind you? I think those are reparations enough, but I'll sweeten the deal a little," Chance suggested. He laid a thumb drive on the nightstand.

Romano was intrigued by the offer. "What's that?"

"It's a million bucks. That should be plenty of reparations."

"Fine. It pays for the men you killed. That debt is now settled." The boss picked up the thumb drive. "Now, I must seek reparations for my son," Edward Romano insisted and stood from the bed.

"I told you I didn't kill him."

"I know. You can go now," Romano stated as he put his robe on. He lit a cigar and walked Chance into the living room area, where he found his men tied up and struggling to get loose.

"Disappointing," the boss mumbled right before the suite door burst open with his nephew Rico leading the charge.

Rico raised his gun and moved toward Hardway with the men from the elevator close behind him.

"Stop!" Romano ordered.

"Uncle, he's the man you've been after."

"No, he's not. There's someone else I'm after. I want you to walk this man out of the hotel and make sure nothing happens to him."

"How do you know?" Rico asked in protest.

"This man walked through this hotel, took out five of our men without firing a shot, and could have killed me anytime he wanted. He could have ended it here moments ago, but he did not. Now, do as I've asked!" Romano turned and walked back into his room. Before closing the door, he looked at Hardway once more. "Stay away from the Russians for the next few days."

"I'll see what I can do," Chance replied and started for the door with Rico.

"One more thing," Romano stated.

"Yeah."

"I think it goes without saying, but I expect that you're done with your business in Philly, and I won't be seeing you back there."

"I don't have any plans to visit the City of Brotherly Love anytime soon."

Edward Romano Sr. looked the man over once more. "Make sure you don't."

"I understand," Chance said and followed Rico out of the room.

Before leaving the Tease, Chance returned to the kitchen and found the hotel security guard to return his suit to him. The man was angry, as anyone would be. Still, Rico persuaded the security guard to take the thousand dollars he had been offered to forget the whole thing. By the time Chance got back to the car, the sun was rising. He was tired, but there was still a lot to be done. Chance got into the car and took out his phone. He called Freddy and waited for the man to answer. He needed confirmation that everyone was still where they were supposed to be, where Chance needed them.

By the time Maxim came out of his room, the sun was up, and Pavel was sitting at the table enjoying some biscuits. Boris sat in a chair with a cup of coffee in one hand and his cell phone in the other, talking to someone. Maxim's shoulder still hurt, but he was able to move it. The bullet he took in Chicago was a reminder he had gone too far to turn back now, though he had thought about it more than once. He had just enough money to escape the Bratva and start life anew, but if he was going to do it, he had to do it now.

Pavel looked up and saw Maxim standing in the living room. "Maxim, good morning. Come have some tea and biscuits with jelly."

"Yes, it looks delicious. I hope there is enough left," Maxim joked as he sat across from Pavel.

"Of course; I have warm ones here for you. Here take some." Pavel lifted the steel compote cover, revealing the fresh warm biscuits that were inside.

Maxim took out one of the biscuits and laid it on his plate. He was pleased to see the glass jar that held the jelly. "Is this—"

"Yes, Maxim. Boris got it from Russia," Pavel excitedly said as his friend picked up the Russian jelly jar. "Yes, my brother.

194

Boris spoils us." Pavel laughed aloud, followed by Maxim. The two men enjoyed the small memento from the Motherland.

Maybe this is where I'm to be, Maxim thought and took a bite of the jelly-covered biscuit Pavel had prepared.

Chance drove to the intersection of Tropicana and Arville, where Freddy had arranged to have something left in the parking lot of a local convenience store. Chance had a plan, and what Freddy left there for Chance to pick up was part of that plan. He already had something of value, but he needed something more to bargain with. The thumb drives with access to money were one thing. Still, he wasn't sure they were enough to guarantee Morgan's safety, especially since the Muñoz Cartel already knew about her. If there was anything else that Chance could count on, it was that Leontii Adamovich couldn't be trusted, and most likely, neither could any of the Bratva.

As he pulled into the parking lot, he drove toward the white-paneled truck with the words "Larry's Linen" displayed on the side in red lettering. He parked next to it and got out, then cautiously looked around. He had already moved on the Romanos, and in a place like Las Vegas, word would have already gotten around that Chance Hardway, the man with a bounty on his head, was on the move. He had to be careful. The convenience store had locals pulling in and driving out after they refueled or filled their coffee mugs. The panel truck was perfect for what he needed to do. His plan was to drive to the Winecup Hotel and Casino, kidnap Boris, and get out before anyone knew he was there. Chance had decided to trade Boris and the thumb drives to Ivan for Morgan. He figured having one crazy Russian to deal with was better than having two fighting for control. Chance also knew he had to do it before the Muñoz Cartel got involved.

When Chance reached the passenger door, he opened it

and stepped inside. Then, surprisingly, he heard something or someone milling around in the back. Chance pulled his 9 mm and pointed it at the large cargo area.

"What in the hell are you doing here?" Chance asked when he saw Freddy sitting on top of a large bundle of clean bedding. He had his laptop open on his knees.

"I think things have changed."

"What are you talking about?" Chance asked and shut the door behind him.

"I'll tell you, but first turn on the truck and kick on the air conditioner. It's hot in here," Freddy instructed. He used a towel with a Winecup logo on it to wipe the sweat from his forehead.

"Okay, what's changed?" Chance asked as he sat and started the truck.

"I take it everything went well with Romano."

"Yeah, we worked it out. C'mon tell me what's changed?" Chance asked again, knowing he had a deadline and needed to get things moving along.

"All right! The Muñoz Cartel is planning something big. I'm hearing chatter all over the place. Apparently, some of the cartel's people are getting called to come to Las Vegas. Then someone offered to sell some information on the Muñoz Cartel for ten thousand dollars."

"Who bought it?" Chance asked.

"I did," Freddy answered flatly.

"Good, I'm glad to hear that."

"Well, we're in this, and I was already moving money around to take care of my own problem anyway."

Chance tilted his head and looked at the Underground's owner. "Your problem?" he asked after a second.

"Yeah, I got to take care of someone who knows a little too much about my business—if you know what I mean."

Chance knew Freddy was talking about Candi, the woman

who had betrayed him and the woman he sent away. Now, it seemed Freddy had placed a bounty on her. "I'm surprised. I didn't think you were the kind of guy who would have someone killed, especially someone like her. I mean, she was a snake, but having her killed—"

"No, no. I'm not having her killed. I offered her money to keep her mouth shut and move to someplace extremely far away from Las Vegas. I may have hinted that I would have her killed, but I don't do what you and the other people we're dealing with do. I'm a businessman," Freddy explained.

Chance thought it was interesting how the man didn't acknowledge any part in facilitating the killing of others. After all, he was the Underground owner, a place where people bought and sold information that could—and had in many situations—end the lives of others. "I understand," Chance replied. He wasn't about to call the man on his illogical reasoning, especially since he needed his help. "So, what was the information you bought?"

"The Muñoz Cartel is taking on Ivan Gorky. Apparently, they were promised Morgan, but as you already know, Leontii backed out on that deal. He also kept part of the money they had paid for her."

"Does Ivan know?"

"I don't think so. His plane lands at McCarran International in about an hour."

Chance didn't know what to do. He thought about staying with the plan he had, but if the Muñoz Cartel killed Ivan, Chance was stuck with two of the Bratva fighting for control. Leontii and Boris were men who couldn't be trusted. *Maybe the better plan is to go after Leontii and take Morgan from him at his house,* Chance thought. He was still running through the different scenarios and possibilities in his head when his cell phone rang.

"What is it?" Chance asked quickly.

"They're moving your girl," Earl answered.

"Damn it!"

Leontii sat in the passenger seat, looking out the window and thinking about what he should do. The brigadier was on his way to the airport to meet with his boss. He had been ordered to bring the girl with him. He didn't know what would happen, but whatever it was, it wasn't good. Igor drove the expensive luxury car while Sacha sat in the back next to Morgan, whom he had tied up before leaving.

Sacha didn't say anything. He kept to himself, paying more attention to his phone than anything else.

When Igor pulled out onto the interstate, Leontii turned around to look at Morgan and then at Sacha. "Sacha, when we get to the airport, I want you to stay in the car with the woman. If I give you the signal, you're to kill her, and if she tries to run, you're to kill her as well. I've grown tired of her, and now she can die," Leontii ordered without moving his mouth too much. He looked at Morgan proudly. "Do you understand?"

"Yes, I will kill her," Sacha answered and glanced at her.

Morgan didn't say anything. She just looked at Sacha with concern in her eyes. She had given up on the possibility of getting out alive. Now, she was angry and felt there was no use in keeping quiet.

"I couldn't help but notice you're not smiling. It's like you can't or something," Morgan remarked smugly.

"Yes, jokes. That's what you Americans do in times like this. I understand. That's all you have left."

"All I have left. What do you have left?" Morgan asked and sat forward, closer to the arrogant Russian.

Sacha reached out and placed his arm in front of her and lightly pushed her back.

Leontii didn't answer. He knew she was right. There was a

big possibility he could be losing his position and possibly his life. He could very well be walking into his own execution.

Boris and his men were finishing breakfast and reminiscing about the past, when they were mere soldiers of the Bratva in Russia. They talked about scraping by on the leftovers handed down to them by the same type of men they had now become. Each one declared they were better than the ones before them and treated their people much better than they ever had been. Boris was still laughing aloud at a joke that Pavel had told when he received a phone call. Boris excused himself from the table to take it.

"What is it?" he asked.

"Someone's taken the money!" The computer hacker, who called himself SyberSam, informed his employer.

"What do you mean? How much?" Boris shouted into the receiver, but the caller did not answer quickly enough. "How much? Tell me!"

"All of it," SyberSam finally answered.

"Get it back!"

"I can't. He took it all and locked me out."

"You were supposed to be the best."

"No, I said I was one of the best, and so is this guy."

"Then you'll give me my money back that I've already paid you."

"I can't. He took that too," SyberSam reluctantly confessed.

"I will find you and kill you!"

"You'll try, but I'll destroy you before that ever happens. You won't be able to get a cup of coffee when I'm done with you. Now, if you find this guy and get me his computer, I can probably get it back for you."

"How do I know I can trust you?" Boris asked.

"Because I'm still on the phone, you jackass! Call me when you have it," SyberSam answered and hung up.

Boris dropped his hands to his sides and looked out the

window. He was angry. He needed a plan and soon. Suddenly, his phone rang again. He looked down at the caller ID. It was Ivan. Now, he desperately needed a plan, and he needed it soon. He answered the call and listened to Ivan give him instructions.

"Fuck!" Boris shouted after getting off the phone.

"Boris, what is it?" Pavel asked after hearing the shouting and seeing the dissatisfied look on the man's face.

"We seem to have run into a problem. Pavel, I think it's time to put your skills to good use."

Pavel was pleased by what he had just heard. "Now that's something I can get behind," he replied and stood from the table.

"What is your plan?" Maxim asked as he stood next to his friend.

CHAPTER 19
ARRIVALS AND DEPARTURES

C hance and Freddy were still sitting in the box truck, waiting. Chance had a new plan, but he needed help, and he needed supplies. Earl was the first to show up. When he entered the truck, he was introduced to Freddy, made his way to the back, and leaned against the wall. He then looked at Chance. "Two million dollars," he said and lit a cigarette.

"Freddy, make it happen."

"What's the account number?" the large man asked and then wiped the beaded sweat from his forehead.

Earl pushed himself off the wall, dug for his phone in his pocket, scrolled through it, and showed it to Freddy. "To this account."

Freddy looked at the number and transferred the money. "It's done. Now what?" the man asked.

"Now we wait for the other truck," Chance replied.

Earl looked out the back window. "It's here."

"Earl, check it out. Make sure everything we need is inside.

I gotta make a phone call," Chance ordered and then walked out of the air-conditioned truck and into the desert's scorching heat, where he dialed a familiar number and waited for the man to answer.

"It's me. I got a deal for you," Chance said.

Hector Muñoz sat at the table, finishing a late breakfast, when Mariana walked in from outside. He could tell by the way she walked that she was coming in to speak to him about business. The cartel leader just didn't know if it was cartel business or personal business concerning the woman who had killed his son.

"Papá, our source called and said Ivan Gorky would be landing at ten o'clock. After he lands, his plane will taxi to the private hangar area, and he will deplane in hangar thirteen," Mariana explained and sat across from her father.

"Make sure our people are ready."

"They're ready. I'm leaving in a few minutes to oversee everything," she replied.

"Why are you going? Can't Manuel take care of it?"

"Yes, but I think someone needs to watch Manuel."

"Why? Has he done something for you to question his loyalty?"

"Not yet, but—"

Hector stood. He was angry. "No, I don't want to hear it. Manuel has saved my life at least four times that I can count. How many times have you saved my life, Mariana?"

"None, I'm just the one keeping the family business running while you sit around, crying about your precious Juan. You're blind to everything except for your anger toward this woman—a woman who refused to lie down and die for your son. Now, I will protect my family and the business you've built in whatever way I see fit. You just sit here and wait until I get back."

"How dare—"

"How dare what, Papá? How dare I speak to you in such a manner, or how dare I take the controls of the family business from the man who's ruining it?"

"You, I'll—"

"I have no time for this with you right now," Mariana said, ending the argument and walking out.

Hector swiped his arms across the table, knocking the dishes and uneaten food to the floor. "I'm the head of this family!" he shouted to an empty house.

The Winecup Hotel and Casino was lavishly decorated, with everything focusing on Las Vegas and gambling. It was owned by a Russian businessman with ties to the Bratva. Having relations with the Bratva was something most would avoid. Still, if a Russian immigrant needed to borrow money, they'd have to look harder because conventional lending institutions were not as friendly to Russian immigrants as the Bratva. The Gorky family was precisely the lending institution that Abram Balakin had turned to when he needed a little financial help in opening his small hotel and casino. Over the past few years, Ivan Gorky and his Bratva had conducted more business within the Winecup walls than anywhere else in Las Vegas.

Boris and Maxim left the Winecup in plenty of time to meet Ivan at the airport at ten o'clock. As Boris drove, he hoped Pavel would be able to get into position, and after he did, Pavel would then be able to take the shot when he needed him to do so.

Maxim was silent, not saying anything to Boris about the lost money, Ivan coming into town, or the men in the Bratva he had helped kill.

Boris looked at his quiet passenger. "What's on your mind, comrade?" he asked and then looked back at the road.

"Nothing, my friend. I just hope Pavel will be successful when the time comes," Maxim answered. He was lying though. He really wanted to get away from the entire situation. Earlier thoughts drifted back into his mind. *I could just walk away*, he thought.

"Don't worry, we may not have any money to start our new family, but when there's no competition, we won't need it," Boris explained as they pulled through the gate leading to the private hangars.

Maxim looked at the runway and saw the familiar black jet taxing toward hangar thirteen. At the other end was another gate, which led to the public departure area. *There must be a flight leaving within the hour. I could just excuse myself and walk away*, Maxim thought. He visualized himself walking away, leaving the turmoil at his back.

"I hope Pavel's in place," Boris stated and parked along the outside wall of hangar thirteen.

"As do I," Maxim responded and then thought to himself, *I wonder if there's a nonstop flight to Miami.*

Manuel and his men were dressed in airport ground crew uniforms. They walked around the hangar, both inside and outside of it, pretending to be busy with work they knew nothing about, while the real ground crew lay tied up somewhere out of sight. The plan was simple. They were to wait until Ivan had his feet on the ground before they took him.

Mariana sat in her SUV across the way, watching everything from the comfort of the rear seat. As she watched and waited, she thought about what she had said to her father. She was ashamed. *He's an old man, and he wasn't supposed to outlive his son. I should have been less adversarial,* she thought and looked out of the dark-tinted window toward the hangar at the black jet pulling inside.

Chance sat inside the white-paneled food delivery truck with the words Air Meals Delivery written on the side. The new panel truck was better suited for the airport. Chance also liked it better than the truck he had left Freddy sitting inside of in the parking lot near the departure terminal. Somehow, Freddy had made a call and was given a special parking permit by a "friend" working at the airport. The old truck was now their command center. The new meal delivery truck provided Chance with a larger front windshield to look out of as he sat and watched the black jet taxiing to hangar thirteen. He had his gear on and was ready to move when the opportunity presented itself.

"Do you have a view inside the hangar?" Chance asked over the radio.

"Yeah, I can see everything, but depending on how the pilot parks, it may change my point of view," Earl replied. The trained sniper sat on the rooftop of a second terminal out of sight of wandering eyes.

"You see anything interesting from up there?" Chance asked.

"Yeah, there seems to be a lot of Hispanics working around the hangar," Earl answered.

"I don't know if that's suspicious or not. I mean, there are a lot of Hispanic people living in Las Vegas," Chance replied.

"No, wait. How many do you see, Earl?" Freddy asked.

"Ten, maybe twelve. Why?" Earl asked as he adjusted his rifle scope.

"Well, the population of Las Vegas is roughly sixty-one percent Caucasian and about thirty-three percent Hispanic. So, it stands to reason that the airport employees should have some non-Hispanic people," Freddy explained.

"Interesting," Earl said and adjusted his rifle's scope. He increased the magnification to get a better look. When he focused on one specific man, he noticed a tattoo on his neck.

"Does a tattoo of a revolver next to a skull mean anything to anyone?"

"Yes! The gun with the skull represents he's a member of the Muñoz Cartel. Do you see any others like that?" Freddy asked.

Earl examined as many of the people he could see. "Yeah, I can confirm that about half are inked up," he answered after a few moments.

"The cartel is coming for Ivan," Chance announced.

"What do you want to do?" Earl asked and then readjusted the scope and got ready to start shooting cartel members.

"I don't know. Just hold for now, and let's see how this plays out."

The pilot slowly eased the jet under the hangar and radioed hospitality to inform them they were ready for the airplane to be cleaned and restocked with supplies. The jet owner expected to leave within the next twenty-four hours, and he wanted the plane ready to go when he was.

"Do you see anything or anyone?" Ivan asked Michail, who was peering out the side window. The trusted man had his 9 mm submachine gun on his side. Michail and the six men he had brought with him were all trained with the military-style weapon, and they all wore a bulletproof vest and tactical gear. They were ready for whatever presented itself when they stepped off the plane.

"No, nothing. Just some airport employees working in the hangar."

"Do you see Romano's people?"

"No, not yet."

Igor pulled in through the gate area and parked next to Boris and Maxim. The Bratva members nodded at each other and exited their cars. Boris looked around for Pavel but didn't see him. He didn't know if that was a good or bad thing. Maxim closed the passenger door and also looked around for Pavel. Still, just as Boris discovered, he could not find the talented killer.

"Good morning, Boris," Leontii announced as he walked to his friend. "I did not expect to see you here."

"I did not either. Ivan called and asked that Maxim and I come here to meet his plane," Boris nervously explained and once again looked around for Pavel.

"You brought Maxim as well. How are you, my old friend?" Leontii asked as he embraced the anxious man.

"I'm well, comrade."

"Igor, look here, our friend has been injured," Leontii announced to his bodyguard as he pointed out Maxim's shoulder injury.

"I see. Now he's a true man of the Bratva," Igor said and looked around at his surroundings. He had a feeling that both Boris and Maxim were acting oddly.

"Brigadier, what has happened to your face?" Maxim asked with false concern in his voice.

Leontii walked back to his car and opened the back door. "That would be the work of my travel companion," the man answered and pulled Morgan from the car.

Sacha, who had not gotten out with the other two men, finally stepped out. He, too, carefully looked around.

"The whore who belongs to Hardway?" Boris asked more than stated.

"Yes, she is furious like the black grizzly of Russia. Do not stand too close," Leontii joked and then pushed his hostage back inside the car.

Chance and Earl stayed in place. They were waiting for either the Russians or the Muñoz Cartel to make a move. Things seem to be moving as expected until Chance spotted Morgan standing next to Leontii Adamovich and his men.

"Do you have Morgan covered?" Chance asked desperately.

"I see her, and I've adjusted for distance and windage. She's dangerously close if things get twisted. I'm good, but they're all pretty close to her."

"Okay, wait. But if someone looks like they're moving on her, you got a green light."

"What about the sleeper?" Freddy asked.

Ivan Gorky stood behind his men and got ready to exit the plane. He took out his phone and called Leontii. The pakhan wanted to make sure his men were in the hangar before he got out. Edward Romano had sounded genuine when he spoke to him on the phone. Still, there was a small chance he'd had a change of heart and was now ready to go to war.

"Ivan, we are just about to come into the hangar," Leontii stated before his boss could say anything.

"Good, we will wait until you get here before we come out. I want you to make sure there are no problems awaiting me," Ivan explained.

"I understand. We will come inside," Leontii replied and used his hand to give Igor the signal to open the trunk. Igor walked to the back of the car and opened the spacious trunk, revealing an arsenal of weapons.

"Boris, Maxim, please come here and choose a weapon," Igor offered and stood back to allow the men to look at the impressive metal lying inside.

"Igor, you have good taste, my friend." Maxim reached in and removed an MP5. The gun was a little shorter than a typical assault rifle but much easier to handle with one arm. Boris reached in and took out an AK-47.

"Nothing sounds better than the sound of a fully automatic AK-47 when it's fired at your enemies," Boris joked and took out one more fully loaded magazine out of the trunk and placed it in his pocket.

Leontii chose to carry the pistol he already had on him, but Igor agreed with Boris and chose the other AK-47. The brigadier ordered Sacha to stay in the car for now and not to leave the girl, then the four armed Russians made their way into hangar thirteen. When they got to the open hangar, Leontii pointed at Maxim. "Stay here. I'll let you know when I'm ready for the woman."

"Okay," Maxim replied and positioned himself so that he had a view of Leontii and Sacha.

Manuel signaled for his men to get ready when he saw the four armed men approaching. He then heard the door latch on the plane pop open. "Wait until I go first," he ordered his men through the wireless mics. The cartel lieutenant looked across the way at Mariana sitting comfortably in the SUV surrounded by her three-man protection team.

"Chance, it's time," Freddy announced.

"All right. I'm moving toward the hangar," Chance said as he moved the truck forward toward the hangar. He wore a baseball hat to cover his face and kept his head down as he got closer to the metal building.

When Leontii entered the hangar, he paused and briefly looked at the men working inside. He then started toward the plane once more as it opened. The first man he saw standing in the doorway was Michail, Ivan's trusted bodyguard.

"Do you see Ivan Gorky?" Mariana asked.

"No, not yet," Manuel answered.

"Wait until he gets out! Don't be in a rush," Mariana instructed.

"I know what I'm doing!" Manuel said out of frustration.

Michail stepped through the door and onto the stairs that one of the ground crew had placed at the door. Ivan's bodyguard was cautious. He turned and looked back at his boss. "Wait until I know it's safe," he instructed.

Ivan did as he was told and moved out of the way to allow two more men to exit first.

Chance had unloaded a metal cart used to load and unload food from the plane from the rear of the truck. He pushed it in the direction of the jet's door while keeping his head down. When he reached the fuselage, he stopped.

The Russians greeted each other, and Michail signaled Ivan to come out of the plane. Leontii gave Maxim the go-ahead to have the woman brought into the hangar. Leontii knew he had made some bad choices, and the woman was his peace offering to his boss. The brigadier still had hopes of trading Morgan for the thumb drive.

Manuel and his men had waited a long time underneath the desert sun for the Russian boss to arrive, and now there he was, walking down the stairs.

Chance took his time and made it look as though he knew what he was doing. He remained by the metal cart and bent over to act as though he was preparing to unload it. When he looked up, he saw Morgan being escorted into the hangar.

"Okay, here we go. I got overwatch. You now have the objective," Earl declared as he changed from one role to the other. He no longer had the job of protecting Morgan. Chance did. Earl was to concentrate his sniper fire at the men who tried to stop Chance from getting her out of harm's way.

"I'm ready," Chance announced.

Earl kept his eye on the man next to Morgan. He was waiting for a signal, and without warning, he saw it. He smiled and spoke into the mic. "Our sleeper is in."

"Good," Chance replied. He looked at the man standing next to Morgan and gave him a slight nod.

Sacha reciprocated the unknown man's head gesture. Sacha had served in the Russian Armed Forces many years ago, which was where he met an odd but gifted Green Beret sniper. The two men trained together for over a year in Europe. Over the years, they had stayed in contact with each other, and when Sacha moved to Las Vegas with the Bratva, he and his old friend Earl reunited. Sacha had seen all the text messages coming in over the last few days through the Underground about Hardway and Morgan. Sacha, who was already questioning his continued employment with the Bratva, reached out to his old friend and asked if he knew anything about the text messages. By luck, he did, and it created a two-million-dollar opportunity that Sacha couldn't turn down.

Chance kept his eye on the man who looked at him and then glanced in the direction behind the food delivery truck. Chance understood what he was hinting at. No matter what happened in the next few minutes, he and Morgan would be moving behind the truck, and Chance needed to cover them when they did so.

Leontii stepped forward, took Ivan by the hand, and kissed his cheeks. "Welcome, comrade."

"Leontii, I don't know if this is a meeting where you'll be happy to see me. I've heard very upsetting things," Ivan said immediately. He wanted his brigadier to know he wasn't happy about being in Las Vegas.

CHAPTER 20
DEAD MAN'S HAND

Leontii had heard what Ivan said, but instead of saying anything, he just stood there for a moment thinking about it. Leontii was the one who oversaw everything in Las Vegas, Chicago, Philly, and California. He had been successful at doing so. He took it as a personal insult that Ivan had not recognized or acknowledged his other successes.

"What has happened to your face? Another failure, I presume," Ivan stated.

"Yes," the brigadier answered. He wanted to lash out but didn't have the manpower to overtake the trained men Ivan had brought with him.

Ivan walked around the man, looking him over. "Where's the money, Leontii?" he asked after making a complete circle.

"I don't have your money yet, but this woman is the one who can get it back for you."

Ivan shook his head, disappointed. "My money? You think it's all my money?"

"Yes, if not you, then who does it belong to?"

"It belongs to me and everyone else in the Bratva," Ivan explained as he began circling the brigadier once more. "Michail uses it to pay for his mother's treatments at the hospital. Igor here probably uses his part to buy his favorite vodka and to pay for whores. It even belongs to you, Leontii."

Mariana watched Ivan Gorky and was happy to see him. She was even more pleased when she saw the woman taken from the car and brought into the hangar. Mariana recognized her from the video. She was the woman who had killed her brother, Juan.

"Manuel, the girl! She's the one we're after! Take her!" Mariana said into the radio.

Manuel looked around at his men. They all heard what Mariana had said through their somewhat concealed headphones. He turned his head away from the men gathered close to the plane and pulled his microphone out from his sleeve.

"When I go for the girl, everyone else takes your man as planned. We stick to the close-quarter maneuver we've practiced in the past," Manuel ordered.

The plan was simple. Each man was to identify the closest target to them, and that was the man he was to engage first. The plan relied on each man knowing where their own people were and judging the enemy who was closest to them as well.

"Diego, when I go for the girl, you kill the man who walked off the plane first. He looks to be the most skilled," Manuel ordered his best friend—and the cartel's best man with a gun.

"Got it!" Diego answered. He usually would be ready for a gunfight, but he and four of the other men were out late drinking until just a few hours ago. Now, he and those men were not at their best. Diego felt sick, hungover, and tired.

Chance waited and listened to some of the conversation between Ivan Gorky and his brigadier. He was also waiting for the right moment to make his move. He needed to make sure Morgan was out of harm's way.

Boris was not saying anything. He knew their conversation

could very well lead to his promotion. He didn't need to take out the head of the family. Boris just needed Ivan to demote or kill the current brigadier and promote him in his place. Boris was feeling much better than before and didn't think he would have to signal Pavel. Once again, he looked around for his trusted assassin but couldn't find him. He did, however, see something that caught his attention. One of the ground crew was wearing an earpiece with a cord running down his neck and into his overalls. He also had a tattoo of a skull and revolver on his neck under the cord. Suddenly, everything seemed to move very slowly. One of the ground crew came running toward Boris and Leontii.

"Ambush!" Boris yelled, and in a fraction of a second, the hangar burst into an eruption of gunfire.

Chance didn't have time to pull his AR-15 from the bottom of the cart when the shooting started. He just ran toward Morgan, who was being carried to the back of the delivery truck by the sleeper, Sacha. When he saw she was safely behind the truck, Chance smiled but dropped to the ground unexpectedly. He felt pain on his right side, around his lower back. It was a familiar pain, one he had experienced before. Chance had been shot, and he knew it, but he also knew it wasn't that bad. He quickly assessed the wound and found the bullet had gone straight through.

Boris turned and fired his gun at the oncoming man. Manuel fell to the ground with a bullet in his shoulder, while Diego and the others tried to take out their assigned targets.

Michail was the second man to shoot. True to what Manuel had said, the skilled Russian took down Diego and two other men before any of them could get off a shot. Maxim did not try to shoot anyone. He ran out of the hangar toward the public departure terminal he had seen when he first arrived. He wanted no part of the Bratva or anyone else like them, including Boris, the man who wanted to be the new pakhan.

Leontii and Igor were in the fight and taking cover behind a large pallet of airplane parts. While Igor provided cover with his AK-47, Leontii looked for his hostage but couldn't find her.

"Get to Sacha and make sure he still has the woman," the brigadier ordered over the gunfire.

Igor nodded and ran toward the back of the delivery truck where he had seen Sacha dragging the woman toward when the shooting started.

As the firefight continued, Chance was able to make his way to some barrels of water where he took cover. He looked around for the sleeper and Morgan. He found them still behind the delivery truck, where Sacha was untying her. Chance started to run out from behind the barrels, but he was forced back behind them when gunfire peppered the ground in front of him. "Damn it!" he yelled and then called his overwatch. "Earl, do you have Morgan?"

"Yes, she and our sleeper are behind the delivery truck, but they can't get out."

"All right, keep her covered. I'll see what I can do from here," Chance said and then slowly maneuvered around to the other side of the barrels. His side hurt, but it was bearable. When he peered out to the right, he spotted a familiar face. Leontii was hiding behind a nearby pallet with his back toward him. Chance needed a gun, and Leontii had one. He took the opportunity and ran from behind the barrels toward the brigadier. Leontii wasn't ready for the attack. He was hit hard and driven into the pallet of parts. The gun Leontii held was forced from his hand, and it slid across the concrete floor into the open field of fire.

Chance maneuvered himself until he was on top of Leontii. He delivered blow after blow to the man.

Leontii reached his arms up to protect his face, and that was when he saw the wound on Chance's side. The brigadier drove his thumb into the open wound. Chance winced in pain and grabbed Leontii's hand to pull it away from the wound. It created an opportunity for Leontii to push Chance off him.

Michail ordered his men to cover him while he moved closer to Ivan. Ivan was under the plane behind the stairs that had been placed against it. The crime boss wasn't afraid, as he had been in many gun battles before this one. He was just unarmed and couldn't fight back.

"Michail!" he yelled when he saw his man.

Michail heard his name and immediately made his way to his pakhan. He grabbed at him and quickly looked him over. "Are you injured?" Michail asked after not finding a wound.

"No. I need a gun, and we need to get out of here."

Michail took the pistol from his side and handed it to Ivan, along with two fully loaded magazines. He then whistled for his men. From what he could see, he had three men still in the fight. When those men heard the whistle, they made their way to the stairs where Michail and Ivan were taking cover.

Manuel crawled to an airplane wing sitting on the concrete floor. He hid under it, knowing it would not provide any protection from a bullet, but it would hide him from view. Manuel then looked around the hangar at his men who were still shooting at the Russians. He also had a view of the dead men lying on the floor.

"Mariana, we can't get to the woman. Bring your men and help us!"

"No, this is on you, Manuel. You have failed." Mariana saw her men dying, yet she did nothing to help, nor would she. This was an opportunity to be rid of Manuel once and for all. "Take me back," she ordered her driver and turned off the radio.

Earl kept his eye on Sacha and Morgan. He tried to figure out a way to get them out of there. The situation was bad. He couldn't get Morgan and Sacha out any more than he could get Chance out of there. They needed a miracle. He was still looking for a way out when he heard someone behind him. He spun around quickly and found a man in a suit holding a sniper rifle as well.

"Who are you?" Pavel asked as he pointed his rifle at the man whom he had discovered in his position.

Earl looked the man over, and when he heard his thick Russian accent, he knew who he was with. "I'm just up here enjoying the show," Earl replied as he held his rifle at his waist. The precision rifle Earl carried was heavy, just as all .50 caliber rifles were, a little too heavy to try to lift it for a kill shot at the man who had the jump on him. He quickly ran through his options in his mind.

In the hangar, Leontii got to his feet and found a metal bar among a pallet of parts, then began hitting Chance with it. Chance tried to protect his body. It was no use. The bar was solid but light enough for Leontii to wield it like an ancient barbarian on some battlefield in a far-off land during a time long ago.

"You thought you could kill me!" the brigadier proclaimed as he paused to catch his breath.

Chance was hurt, but he still lifted himself up to his feet as bullets ricocheted around the two men. Chance was unsteady, and the wound on his side was still bleeding. His head was hemorrhaging blood with every beat of his heart. The bar that Leontii used was a lethal weapon. "You haven't won yet," Chance declared and prepared himself for another attack. Leontii did not disappoint. He went at Chance with the bar once more, but this time, the former Green Beret was ready. Chance stepped into his attacker and spun into the man, grabbing at his head as he did so.

Leontii wasn't prepared for the maneuver, nor was he prepared for what happened next. Chance placed his fingers into the brigadier's mouth and abruptly pulled at the already-injured cheek, ripping it completely open from his lip to his ear. Leontii screamed and dropped to his knees, dropping his weapon in the process. He tried to close the wound with his hands, but it was no use. The wound was too large.

Chance slowly walked over and picked up the bar. Leontii turned to face the man and held his hands up. Chance brought the bar down hard on top of the man's head, killing him.

When Chance turned around, he saw Ivan and his men moving out of the hangar toward the delivery truck while still shooting at the few remaining cartel fighters. Igor was slowly making his way toward the back of the truck as well. The sleeper and Morgan would soon be in the Russian's crosshairs once more. Chance looked up at the building top where Earl was supposed to be, and through the blood that ran down his face, he saw two men, which wasn't good.

Boris, who was still alive, tried to make his way across the open hangar to Ivan and the other Bratva. When he got to the stairs, he stopped to reload, and that was when he saw Chance Hardway standing there unarmed. Boris raised his AK-47 and aimed the assault rifle at the man.

Chance looked over and saw the man aiming his gun at him. He reached into his pocket and removed something from it. Boris smiled and pulled the trigger. A couple of rounds found Chance. The rounds put him on the ground.

Morgan, who was finally free, looked over and saw Chance fall to the ground after he was shot. She screamed and started for him, but Sacha grabbed her and held her in place.

Chance looked back at Boris, who was smiling. Chance smiled back. It confused Boris, but he soon understood why the man was smiling.

Chance looked at Morgan once more and winked. He then looked at Sacha and lifted something higher for him to see. Sacha knew what Chance held in his hand. He turned and threw Morgan to the ground and covered her body. It was the last thing Chance could do. He held aces and eights, the dead man's hand, and it was time to play his hole card. Chance detonated the explosives that he had hidden inside the metal cart next to the plane.

The explosion wasn't a large one, but the jet fuel inside the plane's fuselage made it much bigger than Chance had planned. Flames shot fifty feet into the sky. The fire ran across the hangar's open floor until they escaped the confines of the metal building. The men inside, who were still alive, ran screaming from the hangar and rolled along the ground, trying to extinguish the flames consuming them. The men closest to the explosion died immediately, which included Boris and a few cartel fighters.

Pavel was surprised by the thunderous blast and looked up and away from the man he had found on the rooftop. Earl heard the explosion, but he didn't turn around to look at it. He took advantage of the distraction to raise his .50 caliber at the man who had walked up behind him. Pavel didn't hear the trigger being pulled, the firing pin striking the primer, or the bullet exiting the large-bore rifle.

The unexpecting Pavel didn't even feel the round pass through his body, nor did the impact send him backward, as portrayed in movies. Instead, he dropped to his knees and fell onto his back.

When the man dropped, Earl gathered his equipment and made his way to the hangar.

Morgan and Sacha felt the heat from the flames but were not directly impacted by the explosion. The delivery truck had shielded them. As Morgan started to stand, she saw Ivan and one of his men running toward the parking lot outside the fenced-in airfield. She quickly turned her attention back to where she had seen Chance and saw him still lying on the ground with flames covering his legs. "Help me!" Morgan screamed at Sacha and ran toward the burning man.

Sacha grabbed a tablecloth from the hospitality truck and

followed her. When Morgan reached Chance, she used her bare hands in a frantic attempt to extinguish the flames. Sacha threw the tablecloth over the man's legs and was successful in putting out the fire. Morgan threw herself over Chance and cradled his head in her partially burned hands.

"Please help him!" Morgan begged when Earl arrived by her side. All of them could hear the sirens blaring off in the distance and getting closer.

"We need a car!" Earl declared and started looking around. Finally, he saw a white-paneled truck heading in their direction.

Freddy pulled up and opened the back. "Get in!" the large man ordered.

Earl and Sacha loaded the barely alive Chance Hardway into the truck, where Morgan held him in her lap as Freddy sped out of the airport. They passed countless emergency vehicles on the interstate that had been dispatched to the fiery scene at the airport hangar.

Chance fell in and out of unconsciousness all the way to the hospital. When they finally arrived at the emergency entrance, Sacha and Earl lifted him and carried him out of the truck. Morgan started to follow but was stopped by Freddy.

"You can't go in there. None of us can. The police will be here in a few minutes, and none of us can be here when they do."

Morgan held Chance's hand. She then bent down and kissed him. "I love you," she whispered and let him go.

Sacha and Earl took Chance inside and laid him on a gurney in the hallway. When the hospital staff tried to speak to them, they ran back out to the truck. They climbed back inside, and once again, Freddy sped out of the area.

Sergeant Parker Denton walked around the carnage that laid about and around the burned-out hangar. He was shadowed by two men from the FBI's local office and one ATF agent. The men walked the scene, looking at the dead men who were either shot, burned, dismembered, or a combination of the three.

"What are you thinking?" one of the FBI agents asked.

"I think these cartel guys and these Russians had one hell of a battle," Parker answered.

"How do you know they're cartel and Russians?" the ATF agent asked.

"Well, that's Ivan Gorky's jet—well, what's left of it—and that tattoo on that arm over there is for the Muñoz Cartel," Parker explained.

"Why do you think they were here?" the second FBI agent asked.

"I don't know. Maybe by 'chance,' but it's anyone's guess," Parker stated as he reached into his pocket and held the thumb drive that had been delivered to his office by courier right before getting the call at the airport. The delivery wasn't a surprise. After all, Chance had told him it would be part of the deal when they had spoken earlier.

EPILOGUE
ON A BEACH

The incident at the hangar made international news, and the explosion was captured on a few cell phones by people who were unlucky enough to be in the area. The unstable and blurry amateur videos and images were played and replayed on media outlets around the world. The airport security director claimed that cameras around the hangar had been hacked by an outside source. The unknown hacker deleted all video and surveillance images for the past three months, including the day of the explosion.

Mariana and her father, Hector, flew back to Colombia out of Los Angeles immediately following what Mariana described as a fiasco beyond imagination. She placed the entire failure on Manuel and his plan. However, she neglected to tell her father that she had given Diego and the other men the night before off. She was also the one who gave the men the money they spent getting drunk before the morning assault. During the flight, Mariana took comfort in knowing that the Muñoz family would soon be getting back to doing what they were known for: selling and distributing cocaine around the world. She looked out the cabin window and saw another plane soaring through the bright-blue sky to an unknown destination. She imagined the plane and its passengers were going somewhere exciting and exotic. *It would be nice to take an extended break on a beach somewhere far away from my life, the cartel, and my father,* she thought before drifting off into a deep sleep.

Maxim purchased a seat in economy, as there were no others available on such short notice. Besides, this particular flight was the first flight allowed to fly out of McCarran International Airport after the explosion at one of the airport's private hangars. The Russian's seat and his destination options had been limited. He shook his head in dissatisfaction as he sat between one overweight woman and one hyper teenager who seemed to be making it a point to bump into the man's injured shoulder. Maxim closed his eyes and wondered what the weather would be like in Des Moines.

Ivan and Michail made their way to San Diego, where they boarded a freighter on its way to Asia. They pretended to be part of the crew and used their fake passports to get around the international roadblocks. The FBI was looking for both the Muñoz Cartel and the Bratva after discovering that the plane in the hangar, where many people had died, belonged to the Russian crime boss, Ivan Gorky. The three-week trip would give the pakhan time to figure out what had happened, who was there, and why. He wanted everyone who had crossed him, and he was determined to find them, no matter the cost.

The last couple of weeks had been difficult for Morgan. She couldn't see Chance, and she had to stay out of sight. All she knew was that Chance had gone through a twelve-hour surgery, been placed in an induced coma, and had a severe concussion. Morgan and the others hid in a vacation home in a private gated community that Freddy had acquired. He'd also had a doctor come by the house to treat Morgan's injuries. At Earl's request, Sacha stayed with Morgan and Freddy in the house, allowing Earl to snoop around the hospital where

Chance was staying. Freddy did what he did best. He hacked into the airport and the hospital security cameras and deleted the past recordings. From what Freddy could tell, there was nothing that could lead the feds back to them.

Sergeant Parker Denton spent the last week assisting the FBI, ATF, and other federal law enforcement agencies as they examined everything found in the hangar. The federal investigation into what had happened was going nowhere. The feds knew Ivan Gorky's plane was the one found in the hangar and that he may or may not have been on it when it arrived that day. The bodies of Boris Yelchin and what was left of Leontii Adamovich were found inside the hangar. There was a badly burned body found near the delivery truck, which had subsequently been reported as stolen. That body was that of a Russian named Igor Bortsov. After the explosion, a helicopter pilot, who'd had to make an emergency landing near the burned-out hangar, saw what he believed to be a body on top of a roof. After a search, airport security found the body of a Russian man named Pavel Petrov on top of a roof, along with his sniper rifle that had not been fired.

It was two o'clock in the morning on a Wednesday, two weeks after the airport incident. The story had lost its traction. The media seemed to have forgotten about anything concerning Russians and Colombian cartels. The halls in the hospital where Chance was recovering were somewhat empty. Morgan walked in wearing nursing scrubs and an ID that granted her access to locked doors. She took an elevator to the intensive care floor and got off. She walked past the nurses' station toward room 506. No one stopped or even questioned her as to why she was there. Freddy and Earl had practiced with her countless times until she looked like a nurse, acted like a nurse, and was confident in her ability to present herself as a nurse. When Morgan got to room 506, she paused, took a deep breath, opened the door, and walked inside.

The room was dark and quiet, except for the glow of the lights and soft beeps coming from the equipment connected to the patient lying in bed. At first, she didn't recognize the unshaven man who lay helpless and connected to the monitors, but she could see it was Chance as she got closer. She gasped when she saw how severe his injuries were. She ran her hand along his arm, leaned over, and kissed his lips. A few tears ran down her cheek and fell onto his. "I love you," she whispered.

"He's going to be okay," Parker said from the corner of the room. He had been sitting in a chair in the dark and fallen asleep before Morgan's arrival. He awoke a few moments after she walked in.

Morgan did not turn around to face the man. "I think so too."

"It's hard to believe someone could survive three gunshot wounds, a severe concussion with a brain bleed, a broken jaw, a cracked orbital, and third-degree burns that required a few skin grafts. Not to mention the cuts that required countless sutures to close," Parker explained from the chair. He made no attempt to stand.

Morgan cried a little more but did so quietly as she looked at Chance. "Yeah, he's a strong man."

"Do you know why he went through all of this?" Parker asked.

"No. Do you?"

"Love."

"Love?"

"Yeah, it seems this woman he loved got herself into some trouble with some awfully bad people. You know, the kind who don't forget. The kind who keeps coming until they settle the score. Do you know the kind I'm talking about?" Parker asked, trying to make a point.

Morgan took a deep breath before answering. "Yeah, I know the kind. Where's this woman he loves now?"

"Don't know. She calls herself Morgan. There's plenty of girls named Morgan in Las Vegas, but unfortunately, I don't have a last name so I can't find a lease, a mortgage, a criminal record, or fingerprints. It's like she never existed. I mean, this Morgan could just walk away, go anywhere, and set up a new life someplace where no one knows who she is or how she came to be there. If she wanted to, I mean."

Morgan put her hand down and held Chance's tightly. "What about him?" Morgan questioned with her voice starting to crack.

"Well, Chance Hardway can't start over. Everyone knows who he is and how to find him. If this Morgan woman is in his life, then he's in danger. The Colombians and the Russians are after her, not him."

"Is he a friend of yours?"

"Yeah, we're friends. I kind of forgot that we were for a little while, but I'm back now," Parker ashamedly confessed.

"You'll make sure he'll be okay, right?"

"That's why I'm here now."

"He'll need friends when he wakes up to get through this."

Parker stood and looked at the man on the bed. "Yeah, he will. Well, I'm going downstairs to get some coffee. You won't be here when I come back in about thirty minutes, will you?" Parker asked, hinting that she shouldn't stay around for long.

"No, I'm leaving," Morgan answered.

"I'm guessing I won't ever see you again."

Morgan wiped her eyes. "No, my time is up. I'm on my way out."

"Good luck then," Parker replied before walking out of the room.

Morgan sat on the side of the bed as tears found their way onto the sheets. Chance didn't move, his breathing was steady, and he looked to be at peace. She ran her hand across the hair that now covered parts of his face. She laughed, knowing it would drive him crazy when he woke up. Morgan took every bit of the thirty minutes Parker had given her. In that time, she talked about her memories and how much she loved him. Occasionally, his pulse rate increased when she touched him.

When it was time for her to leave, Morgan stood, leaned over, and kissed him good-bye. She placed her head on the side of his and whispered, "I love you," then stood back up and saw that Chance's eyes were open. He didn't say anything. He just looked at the woman he loved. Morgan was surprised. She covered her mouth and grabbed his hand. Chance closed his hand around Morgan's and looked into her eyes. "I love you so much!" she said through sobs. She leaned down once more and kissed him before running out of the room.

Chance tried to lift himself but couldn't. He rolled to his left and right as his heart rate increased, bringing the nurses into his room. They attempted to calm him but weren't having any success. Finally, a nurse injected something into his IV line that quickly took effect. Parker returned and saw the end of the commotion. He hurried to Chance's side and heard him say, "Morgan…" right before he went unconscious.

Morgan found Earl in the rental car that he had parked on the first level of the parking garage. She got inside, and the two sped out of the parking lot. Earl didn't know where she was going, nor did he want to know. He had been told by Freddy to take her to a private airport in Henderson. There, she would board a plane waiting to fly her far away from Las Vegas, the Russians, the Colombians, and the love of her life.

"Good luck," Earl said when he stopped near the gate leading to the airfield.

Morgan didn't get out right away. She sat there thinking and then she opened the door. "Take care of him," she said before getting out.

"I will."

The private pilot was waiting at the gate for her. He

escorted her to the plane, helped her get inside, and went through his take-off procedures. After a few minutes, the pilot taxied the small aircraft out to the runway, and a few minutes later, Morgan found herself looking out at the horizon just as the sun was rising.

"I was told you would let me know where we were going when you got on board," the pilot stated and looked at his instrument panel.

Morgan thought about it for a minute. "How far can we fly in this plane?" she asked.

"I can get you to Amarillo and even farther after refueling."

"Amarillo will be far enough. I'll make it on my own from there," Morgan said and opened her purse to look at the thumb drive given to her by Freddy. The large man had told Morgan that Chance had him put a lot of money into a bank account under the name of Abigail Sawyer and to give the thumb drive with instructions on how to access it to her if anything happened to him. Now, she wished Chance were sitting next to her.

Morgan closed her eyes and drifted off to sleep, where she dreamed of another life, a life where she and Chance were together on a beach where they and their children lived, loved, and laughed.

SHOT CALLER

A CHANCE HARDWAY CRIME

ACTION SERIES BOOK 3

PROLOGUE

Rosslyn Jennings kept an eye on the clock. It was twenty minutes before five o'clock on a Friday afternoon, and she had an exciting weekend planned. Henry, her boyfriend, was picking her up after work. They were driving to a cabin where they planned to stay until Sunday afternoon. It was a three-hour trip to the cabin near the town of Black Mountain, and she wanted to leave right after she locked the bank's doors. Rosslyn was a dedicated employee who was committed to the success of Triple Net Investments and Loans. She had worked for the financial institution for over ten years. Through those years, she had been promoted from counter teller to loan officer—and now branch manager. When the bank opened twenty-five years ago, its primary business was in commercial lending and investments. After many successful years, it became a community bank with branches across the United States.

Rosslyn was getting a little nervous as the minutes steadily moved closer to the five o'clock hour. The armored car service the bank used had not arrived. It was ten minutes late. Wheeler Armor was usually on time, but not today.

"Is the armored car coming today?" Emma asked. Emma was one of the bank's tellers and Rosslyn's favorite one. Emma had been with the bank for six months. She was a graduate of the University of North Carolina with a degree in finance. She had become popular with the customers in the short time that she had been with the bank. Emma was tall, blonde, and thin with a curvy figure. She was also the only one Rosslyn trusted to do important tasks and do them correctly. Over the past six months, they had become close. The two of them closed the branch together every Friday. Emma made more money than the other tellers because she took on additional responsibilities.

"Yeah, I guess they're late," Rosslyn answered as she looked toward the door for the familiar black-and-gray metal, squared box on wheels.

"Do you want me to balance my register and close the vault?" Emma asked. She was the only teller window left open. The other tellers left at four thirty, including the bank's security guard, Larry, who had dinner plans. When Larry asked to leave early, Rosslyn was surprised. Larry never left early. The branch manager was even more surprised when Larry told her he had a date. Apparently, Larry had met someone online and this afternoon was the only time that his new possible love interest could meet.

"No, not yet. If they show up late and we close the vault, we'll have to wait for the automatic time delay before it opens again. We'll be here until after six if we do that. Henry and I have the cabin for tonight through Sunday only."

"That's right. The offer expires after this weekend, doesn't it?"

"Yes, they told Henry the prize was only good for this specific weekend."

"I remember now. You told me that on the day Henry won the cabin getaway."

"Yeah, he didn't even remember filling out an entry form. Henry still thinks someone made a mistake, but he received the confirmation in an email, so we're going. I hope we don't have to sit through one of those timeshare presentations," Rosslyn said just as the front doors opened.

"Sorry we're late. The radiator went out on our other truck

this morning, and we had to wait for it to be repaired before starting our pickups," Jerry said as he walked into the lobby carrying an empty bag. He was followed by Enrique, who also held a large bag. Both men were armed, wore bulletproof vests, and were familiar with the bank employees. The last Friday of the month was a hectic day for the two men and their driver, Gary, who remained in the armored car. The three Wheeler Armor security guards made six stops on this particular day every month. Triple Net Investments and Loans was Wheeler Armor's largest client, and their most lucrative. Rosslyn's branch was the smallest of the branches and had the least amount of money to pick up, but the other five were much larger and had a lot of money to be picked up. Now, after all Triple Net Investments and Loans pickups were completed, the three men would be carrying an estimated two million dollars in their truck.

"Hi, guys," Rosslyn said as she made her way toward the vault.

"Hello, ladies," Jerry replied as he walked toward the vault while smiling sheepishly at Emma, whom he had been dating for the past two months.

Emma smiled and flirtatiously waved back at the man.

Gary sat impatiently inside the armored truck, waiting for the others to return. Usually, he would be surveying the area for anything suspicious, but not today. The truck's seat was broken and locked too far forward, pushing his knees against the dash. Gary was irritated. He kept trying to fix the seat release when he should have been watching for anyone approaching the truck. He was still looking down when he heard someone knock on the driver's door. Startled, Gary looked up and then to the side. Next to the door was a man wearing all black, in body armor and a mask, and holding an AR-15.

"Open the door!" the masked man ordered.

"I can't!" Gary yelled back and reached for the truck radio.

He was about to call dispatch when the gunman held a cell phone up to the window. Gary looked at the screen and saw another masked man holding a gun at Cynthia, Gary's wife.

"Open the door, and she'll live," the gunman stated.

Gary reluctantly did as he was told and opened the door. The gunman pulled him out, disarmed him, pushed him to the ground, and zip-tied his hands behind his back. The gunman was Topher 'Top' Wilson. Top went inside the truck and threw money bags from the back out to the ground. When he was finished, he jumped out and surveyed the crowd that had started to gather around. None of them approached the truck.

"Watch him," Top ordered another man dressed in the same manner who had been standing behind the truck. The man knelt over the guard and kept an eye on the people on the street. Top ran toward the bank door where four other masked gunmen waited.

"Thirty seconds in. Two minutes left. Go, Go!" Top ordered after looking at his watch.

Emma was startled when the front doors suddenly and unexpectedly burst open.

"No one move!" Top yelled as he and the four men entered the bank with their guns pointed at the occupants inside. Top's men each made their way to the four people inside and kept them covered.

The bank robbers had a plan. They were prepared, and to Jerry, it looked as though they had rehearsed for the robbery.

"We're not moving," Jerry said after dropping his bag and lifting his hands into the air. "Take the money. No one will try to stop you." He was an experienced security guard and knew it was best to follow the gunmen's commands. Right now, Jerry had to be a good witness. He needed to pay close attention to what the robbers looked like, what they wore, how they stood, what they said, and how they said it. He also didn't want anything to happen to Emma.

"Cover them. I'm going into the vault," Top instructed and then ran into the large safe and started loading the bank's money into his bag.

Jerry looked at each man and made mental notes of them all. *Five men inside and one or two more outside probably.* He thought.

The men who were left watching Jerry and Enrique disarmed them, zip-tied their hands behind their back, and forced them to the floor.

"Which one of you knows how to operate the bank's cameras?" Carter 'Crank' Thomas asked. Crank was a big intimidating man with a short fuse. "Who?" he yelled and pushed Rosslyn backward with the butt of his rifle after no one answered him quick enough.

Rosslyn screamed and started crying.

"I can," Emma said, volunteering herself. "I have to go over there to do it." She pointed toward Rosslyn's office.

"Move, bitch!" Crank ordered and pushed her forward, knocking her down onto her face.

Emma lay there for a moment but then slowly picked herself up off the floor. She turned and looked at the man. Her face was bloody. She was angry and wanted to hurt him but knew she could not. She just turned and started back toward the office with the man following close behind her.

Inside Rosslyn's office, Crank watched as Emma pulled up the video surveillance footage. He ordered her to delete it all. Emma did as she was told and was soon back in the lobby with everyone else.

After Top finished loading the money into his bag, he hurried out of the vault. When he got back into the lobby, he saw the two guards on the ground, along with one of the women. He looked to his right and saw Crank standing next to the other woman; she was bleeding from her face. Top gazed directly at Crank disapprovingly.

Crank saw the look in Top's eyes. He shrugged his shoulders as if the woman's injuries weren't a big deal. Top's other three men were familiar with the gaze. He wasn't happy.

"We got cops coming!" Billy 'Kid' Stevens said over the radio. Kid was the robber who had stayed outside to provide cover while keeping an eye on the guard on the ground.

"Grab her and bring her along," Top ordered Crank.

"No, take me!" Jerry offered as he tried to stand.

"No, lover boy. You wait here," Top stated and then kicked Jerry in the face, breaking his jaw and knocking the defenseless man onto his back.

The five bank robbers made their way to the door and then outside with their hostage in tow. A full-sized black SUV skidded to a stop next to the armored truck. Kid tossed explosives inside the armored truck, dragged the driver to the sidewalk, and climbed into the back of the SUV. He was quickly followed by two of the other robbers that had gone inside. The rear window was open, and the three men got ready for anyone who came up from behind.

Top stood at the passenger door at the ready, while one of his men ran to the other side of the SUV. The two men provided cover until they were prepared to drive away. Crank pushed Emma into the back seat. He then loaded the money bags from the armored car and the bank on top of her, then got in next to his hostage.

"We're in!" Crank yelled. Top and the other man on the other side of the SUV quickly got inside. The driver sped away just as the armored car exploded.

Four hours and two car changes later, Top and the others finally arrived at the cabin deep in the Smoky Mountains. The men quickly began the process of getting things ready to be cleaned.

"You put her inside that one and then blast her," Top ordered as he pointed at Crank.

"Why do I have to do it?" the big man asked angrily.

"Because you're the one who fucked up!"

"Fine!" Crank said in anger as he walked inside the cabin.

"You okay?" Top walked over and asked the hostage.

"Do I look okay? Look at my fucking face!" Emma shouted. Emma's real name was Oliva Moore. Sometimes the guys called her Shot Caller or Boss, but none of them called her Olivia, not because she wouldn't allow it… They just didn't know her real name.

Crank walked back outside carrying Emma's lookalike. He walked to the car and placed her in the rear seat. The big man then covered his face as he placed the shotgun barrel on the side of the dead woman's head and pulled the trigger. Crank knew he had messed up earlier when he broke Shot Caller's nose when he pushed her to the floor in the bank. After he made the lookalike woman's face unrecognizable, he climbed out of the car and walked toward Shot Caller.

"Boss, I'm sorry. I got a little carried away in the bank, and what can I say, I—"

A bullet from Top's gun entered the side of Crank's head, and Crank dropped to the ground.

"Why did you do that?" Shot Caller asked. The man's blood had splattered onto her.

"He fucked up!"

"What do you want us to do with him?" Kid asked while looking down at the dead man.

"Drop him somewhere far away from here. Remove his clothes and burn his body," Shot Caller ordered.

Kid and the other men picked Crank up and put him in the trunk of Kid's car. They then went inside the cabin to get their bags. Ten minutes later, everyone was ready to leave. They gathered around Shot Caller once more.

"Once I get the money to the cleaner, I'll deposit everyone's share. It should take about two weeks. Take these new cell phones and keep them turned on and on you always. If you don't answer when I call, I'll give you ten minutes to call me back. If you don't, I'll assume you've been arrested or you're dead, and I'll replace you. When I find a new job, I'll call you, and you need to be ready to go."

"You got it, Boss," Kid responded and turned back toward his car. The other men got into their cars and drove away.

"Where're you going? You want some company?" Top asked as he followed his ex-girlfriend to her car where she cleaned herself off. He desperately wanted to be with her again.

"No. I told you before that we're through. Like Crank, you fucked up, remember?"

"I guess it's guys like Jerry who are curling your toes. Is he your brand these days?" Top remarked sarcastically.

"Maybe he is. You know, I did like the way he would climb on top of me and fuck me hard and fast, kind of like he did last night."

"Fuck you!" Top said angrily, then turned and hurried away to his car.

Olivia walked to the car where her lookalike was sitting in the back seat. She lit the torch Kid had prepared and stood there looking at the woman. Her body had been on ice in the cabin for three months. Her real name was Sondra Smith; she was a drug addict from New York. Olivia's contact at the coroner's office in New York had called her when the overdose victim came in. The contact described Sondra as "less dead." The term was used to describe people no one would notice as missing or dead in society. The less dead were the homeless, runaways, prostitutes, and drug addicts. Sondra was the same size, build, and had the same hair color as Olivia. Sondra's body had cost Oliva five thousand dollars, but she was worth it. Rosslyn and Jerry would need closure, and believing Emma was dead was the best way to do that. Olivia tossed the torch into the gasoline-doused car and stood there a moment while one of society's throwaways burned.

Olivia got into her car and drove away as black smoke filled the sky. Her car was a white luxury convertible coupe that was fast. As she drove west, Olivia thought about where she wanted to go next. In Augusta, Georgia, she stopped at a light and let the top down after getting gas. She turned the radio on before turning onto Interstate 20.

"Where should I go?" Suddenly, she got her answer. It came from the radio.

"The Emerald Coast Casino in sunny Las Vegas, come stay and play with us."

"The Emerald Coast Casino in Las Vegas, that sounds good to me."

ALSO BY MICHAEL MERSON

Heartbeats of a Killer

The Secrets of Taylor Creek

Roses in the Sand

Jaxson Locke Series Box Set 1-3

Beach Escape

Victim's Advocate Book 1: No Justice

Victim's Advocate Book 2: Revenge

Double Down, A Chance Hardway Crime
Action Series 1

ABOUT THE AUTHOR

Michael grew up in Pensacola, Florida, where he spent the summer months as a youth at the beach, tubing down the river or splashing around in a pool near his grandmother's home. After graduating from high school, he joined the US Army and served in the Military Police Corps. After nearly seven and a half years, Michael left the military. He took a position at the Colorado Springs Police Department, where he served the community for ten years. An injury on duty forced him into early retirement from policing. Currently, Michael is the Department Chair of the Criminal Justice Department at a local community college. Michael earned a Bachelor of Science in Sociology with an emphasis in Criminology from Colorado State University and a Master of Criminal Justice from the University of Colorado.

Michael started his writing career as a ghostwriter for a publisher of textbooks. Eventually, he co-authored a textbook. Michael has always had the desire to write fiction. Through the encouragement of his family and friends, Michael started writing mystery fiction and hasn't stopped. Michael's wife, Stefanie, still catches him daydreaming as he drives down the highway thinking about different stories. The facial expressions that he makes reveal to her that somewhere in his mind, he's reviewing a chapter, scene, or dialogue between characters for a new book.

Made in the USA
Columbia, SC
28 April 2022

59543698R00150